CONVERSATION IN A BELGIAN BAR

by

Robert Rahula

ALSO BY ROBERT RAHULA

NOVELS:

Messieurs
Panamaniac
Island of Misfits
Day Another Paradise In
One Last Fling
Bathhouse Stories
All the Yage in Reno
Exigent Circumstances
Uninvited Guest

SHORT STORIES:

Horror Stories for Children

POETRY:

Trigger Points
Dentro Del Corazón Bloqueada
Camino
Migration
I Sing the Body Politic
Wonderland
From Whose Bourn
Poemas Españoles
Expat Poems

ANTHOLOGIES:

Half Life
The Essential Dan Landes

CONVERSATION IN A BELGIAN BAR
© 2016 by Robert Rahula

www.robertrahula.com

First Printing, 2018
ISBN 978-0-9994736-8-9

Alma-gator Press
Barcelona • Madrid • La Chorrera

"... the end of all our exploring
will be to arrive where we started
and know the place for the first time."

– T.S. Eliot

Chapter 1: Ennui

Well, I guess to answer your question, I would say that you would first have to appreciate what Ricardo's state of mind was last year. He was no longer a young man, you know. And he had grown rather... well, rather weary of life... or maybe it was just that he had grown weary of being himself. He had lived so many years, always doing exactly what he wanted, moving about, accountable to no one, enjoying the type of freedom of choice that only living alone can bring—some would call it a debauched life, I suppose, but I prefer the word satyric. Either way, he had no regrets about any of that. But somehow, last spring, he had grown unaccountably despondent... tired of just being Ricardo. And one day he caught himself saying out loud to himself, *What's wrong with me? What the fuck am I doing? What's happened to my life?*

Hmm... maybe this is a longer story than I thought. Do you have time? Well, bring your glass over here and I'll tell you... Try the other chair, it's more comfortable... How to begin? Well... the month was May, and the rainy season was approaching. You know he'd been living in Panama, right? No, longer than that, maybe for eleven or twelve years now, in a small town in the central valley.

Anyway, as I was saying, it was last May when this... this sense of weariness descended on him. At first he thought it was the season change. The rainy season starts slow in Panama, with just a few clouds in the blue afternoon skies at the beginning of May, then more clouds each day, a few soft showers by mid-month, just *pelo de gato lluvia*, as the locals call it, "cat fur rain", a soft misty rain. But, by the end of the month the cat turns dark and ferocious, and the rains last for one or two hours every day.   Then in June the monsoons come, with torrential downpours lasting eight or nine hours a day. Normally, Ricardo liked the rainy season. He would stock up on coffee and liters of sangria, and sit in his tiny apartment and just write. You knew that about him, didn't you? That's why you asked me about him. You must be a writer, too. Yes, I thought so. It's a good thing to be—a writer—because on some level or other, you're always thinking about the truth of things. Few people do that anymore, you know—think about the truth of things. Most people just babble on and on about useless things, making such a big deal out of their smallest complaints... I really don't like people. Ricardo didn't either. I think that's what I liked about him.

But I digress. As I was saying, last May, Ricardo had grown restless, unaccountably weary of things, even slightly irritable. At first he thought it was the darkness in the afternoon skies that was depressing him. But that wasn't it—he still enjoyed sitting out on his little balcony in the late afternoon after a good day of writing, just sitting there with a cup of coffee or a glass of sangria, depending on the hour, and watching the thick black clouds roll over the distant mountains and march slowly toward the central valley like a massive army. So it wasn't the weather that was making him restless.

Then he thought it must be because he had to return to the states in June.   His passport was about to expire, and even though he had residency status in Panama—a *pensionado residente* card they call it—that residency was dependent on him having a valid passport. He could have renewed it at the U.S. Embassy in Panama City, but his U.S. driver's license was also about to expire and he had to renew that back in New York.

Normally, Ricardo went back to the states once a year anyway, but only when he felt like it. This was different—he *had to* go back last June to deal with these legalities, and it felt like he was being summoned back. Maybe that's what annoyed him... maybe that's why he had been feeling so pissy as the days of May drifted by. But it had to be done, and so he decided he might as well try and get others things done while he was back in the U.S., like meeting with his publisher, his tax accountant, his lawyer, and his stockbroker... more legalities... It seems that the older you get, you know, all your friends die off and you're just left with lawyers and accountants... and that was the case with Ricardo too. He doesn't have too many friends left... and everybody needs a few friends, you know.

But anyway, he did go back to the states... and he did renew his passport... and he did renew his New York driver's license. How? Oh, well, like thousands of other expats, he keeps a legal U.S. address by using a friend's address. Even the most diehard expats have to have a U.S. address for all kinds of legal reasons... Social Security, passports, taxes, investment accounts, bank accounts, et cetera. And so, Ricardo used Phillipe's address. Phillipe was an old transsexual friend in Hamburg, New York, which is where Ricardo used to live before he moved to Panama. It's a small town about twenty minutes outside of Buffalo. They had met there, oh God, decades ago; and so, when Ricardo moved to Panama, Phillipe let him use her address in Hamburg. Any mail that came to Ricardo in New York, she would forward to him in Panama. To thank her, Ricardo always brought her several packages of Panamanian coffee whenever he went back to the states. In fact, it was during Ricardo's visit with Phillipe last June when the idea of visiting Europe began to gel in

Ricardo. And so... to answer your question about what Ricardo was doing in Europe, the story must begin with Ricardo going to see Phillipe in Hamburg, New York.

"Oh, coffee!" Phillipe squealed as Ricardo handed her three two-pound packages of Panamanian coffee. "Thank you! You are soooo sweet to remember."

Phillipe leaned over and gave Ricardo a little kiss. "Come on in, Ricky-boy, come in. Oh it's so good to see you! How long are you in town for?"

"Just a few weeks, maybe less," Ricardo said as he stepped inside. "I had to renew my passport. They're going to mail my new one here. I paid an extra sixty bucks so they would expedite the process. It should come in a week or two. So be on the lookout for a special delivery package soon."

"Oh, no problem, Ricky-boy. You can use me as your mailbox anytime," Phillipe said with a laugh. "Would you like a beer?"

"Phillipe, it's 10 a.m.!" Ricardo exclaimed.

"Oh yes, sorry... a glass of wine then?"

"No, I'm good. Thanks."

"Well, I do have coffee, still hot in the pot. It's not Panamanian, but..."

"Well, yes, coffee would be nice, thank you," Ricardo said.

"Want me to sweeten it for you?" Phillipe sang as she went into the kitchen.

"Please."

Ricardo smiled and shook his head. Phillipe had a way of turning any sentence into a double entendre.

"Cream?" Phillipe yelled from the kitchen.

"No thanks," Ricardo yelled back.

"Are you sure?" Phillipe asked.

"Yes," Ricardo laughed.

Phillipe came back into the room with a cup of coffee and handed it to Ricardo.

"So," Phillipe began, "new passport—how exciting! Planning some great travels?"

"Well, no," Ricardo said. "Just back home to Panama."

"Oh no, Ricky-boy, no no no. You can't get a new passport and just go back to Panama. There will be all those blank pages! What you have to do is travel a whole bunch immediately, get all those pretty stamps! A blank passport is soooo boring."

"Well, you know Phillipe, it's funny you should say that. Because for some reason this morning, I was thinking about going to Spain for a few weeks before returning to Panama. I haven't been back there in years, but lately I've missed it. You know, I like Panama a lot, but I miss the real thing."

"Oh you should, Ricky-boy, but not just Spain. Go see France and Germany, too! Expand your horizons. See Europe while there's still a European Union."

"Ha, yes, well I could spend a couple of days in Berlin—visit the baths and the sex clubs," Ricardo said

"Now you're talking," Phillipe replied "Though you don't have to go to Berlin to see sex clubs. You can get that in Buffalo."

"What do you mean?" Ricardo asked.

"You remember Jimmy's?"

"The gay bathhouse? Of course I do, I remember it well. But I'm talking about male-female sex clubs. They're very big in Berlin now."

"No, no," Phillipe replied. "Jimmy's has gone uptown since you've been gone, sweetie." Phillipe leaned forward and said with a dramatic whisper, "On Sundays, they're co-ed."

"Really?" Ricardo asked, "Co-ed? A co-ed gay

bathhouse... here in the states? Have you gone there? Have you seen this?"

"Of course not, darling," Phillipe replied. "I have no interest in sex with women. But you should check it out and tell me so I know. Take a look at their website. They've been doing that for the past six months."

"Huh... a sex club in Buffalo," Ricardo mused. "Who would've thunk it?"

Anyway, Ricardo and Phillipe talked for a least an hour that day, each sharing what they had been up to the past year. Ricardo didn't volunteer anything about the ennui that he had been feeling lately, but Phillipe must have sensed it, because at one point, she turned to him and said:

"Yes, I think you should definitely go back to Spain, Ricky-boy. It would be good for you. Sometimes we all have to reach down and touch our toes just to realize how much we've grown."

Ricardo smiled and said, "That's an odd metaphor."

"Well," Phillipe continued, "for example, I keep an old suit in the closet, one that I used to wear when I was Ronald, you know, before the surgery. About once a year, I take it out and put it on and look at myself in the mirror, just to realize how much happier I am now, how far I've come. Maybe visiting Spain will make you realize how much happier you are now."

What? Why Spain? Oh, you didn't know that Ricardo was born in Spain? That was the point of what Phillipe was trying to tell him. No, Ricardo's parents were U.S. citizens, but his mother was from Spain, and it just happened that Ricardo was born in Barcelona. Oh no, no, Ricardo is definitely a bona fide U.S. citizen. In fact, he grew up somewhere on the east coast, I believe. But what I was trying to explain was that Phillipe sensed that

Ricardo was somehow despondent, and somehow she intuited that if Ricardo were to go visit the land of his birth, he might somehow connect to something he had lost or maybe realize he hadn't lost it in the first place. The point is that Phillipe really felt that Ricardo should make that trip. And as Ricardo later told me, those words of Phillipe really made an impact on him, maybe even convinced him to book a flight to Europe.

But anyway, that's where the idea to come back to Europe came from—that conversation with Phillipe. It's funny, in a way... you never know what real impact the simple words that you say might actually have on the person you're talking to. I don't think Phillipe actually realized what she had set into motion with her words... Ricardo certainly didn't foresee it, either. He was still just being dragged down by that feeling of being in a rut and needing to do something different, something radically different to shake the ennui he was having. So that night, sitting back in his hotel room, he opened up his laptop and booked a flight to Europe. His intention was to find a cheap flight to Barcelona, where he was born, and from there to take either the ferry or a puddle jumper over to the island of Menorca, where he had lived for so many years...

What? No, no. I said he *grew up* in the U.S., but he had moved back to Spain in his twenties. He lived there for many years, decades actually, both in Menorca and Madrid, before returning to the states. That's when he settled in Hamburg, New York. Of course, that was a long time ago, too. From there he moved to Panama. But it was in Hamburg, New York, that he first started to write and be published. You've read his books? Which was your favorite? Yes, that is a good one. No, I don't think it was a particularly unusual life, living in two different countries. Many people grow up that way, and most do find it enriching. But I do think that somehow it left a mark on Ricardo. I think that in some way he was always searching for a home he never had, maybe for a place that never existed. I think that's what Phillipe sensed in him that day—a yearning to reconnect with something that resembled home.... Who knows? Anyway, as I said, later that night, back in his hotel, Ricardo booked a flight to Europe. He looked for cheap airfare to Spain, but it was the high season there and prices were steep. But he found a relatively inexpensive flight to Amsterdam, and he figured he could take a local flight from there to Spain. He booked the flight out a few weeks so that there would be enough time for his new passport to arrive. He still had a number of appointments in New York City with his tax accountant and his publisher and others that he had to do before going to Europe. Besides, he wanted to check out the co-ed Sundays at Jimmy's bathhouse.

Chapter 2: Jimmy's

By the way, I haven't properly introduced myself. My name is François Rayon. Yes, glad to meet you. You're from the states? Yes, I could tell. And I see your glass is almost empty. Permit me to buy the next round. *Garçon, deux autres, s'il vous plaît.* Where was I? Oh yes, Jimmy's... well, to say that Jimmy's bathhouse was a fluke would be an understatement. As you might imagine, Buffalo, New York, was never a liberal nexus of any sort. But back in the sixties, the city was on hard times, and there was all this abandoned property, and this guy named Jimmy Taltrex came in and made the city government of Buffalo an offer: he wanted to open up a gay bathhouse in this totally abandoned industrial area; and he was willing to pay top dollar for it, *as long as* the city signed a contract stating they would never harass him about the nature of his business. And he spelled out exactly what his bathhouse was all about. Well, the city fathers held their noses and signed it, because they were desperate for any business that would develop their city. Besides, they never thought he would make a go of it... but he did. And even after the seventies came, and then the eighties, and the nineties, and the city became all gentrified, they were stuck with that contract. So they learned to live with it, because Jimmy's kept a very low profile. Even his neighbors never knew what went on there. But the gay and bisexual population did, because when the internet happened... well, Jimmy's had customers from Canada, Ohio, Pennsylvania, you name it. He must have been a visionary, that guy. Way ahead of his time. Rumor had it that he was Mafia, but nobody cared. It was a nice clean gay bathhouse, and when Ricardo was living in Hamburg just down the road, well, he would often use their services.

Now... when I say gay bathhouse... you do know what I'm talking about, don't you? Yes, I thought so. You seem like the kind of person who might know these things. Anyway, Ricardo had been a regular at Jimmy's, but then of course, he moved to Panama, so it had been, what? Almost eleven or twelve years since he had been there when Phillipe told him about their "co-ed Sundays".

It's a funny thing about sex... I think Ricardo would agree with me on this... It's totally mental. Here you had a gay bathhouse... a place where gay men had been gathering for decades to meet safely, out of public view, to sit in the steam room and fondle each other, to select partners and wander off to tiny rooms or dark corners to have sex, and you put two little words in their website: "co-ed Sundays" and suddenly everyone goes ballistic, as if their sanctuary is going to be invaded and ruined by women or couples wanting to do the exact same thing they were doing. It's the mental image of "co-ed" that does it... that one word... and some of Jimmy's customers hated it, and some of them loved it... But the fact of the matter was that for Jimmy's, it was strictly a business decision. After so many years, Jimmy's was simply not the only game in town. The internet took over the porn business; other bathhouses opened up; Canada legalized prostitution; and so, Jimmy's had to adapt. Opening his bathhouse to couples and women on Sundays was strictly a business decision, not a political one. Many of the men who frequent gay bathhouses are not exclusively gay, you know, but bisexual, like Ricardo. And many of them are even married. Many of them are swingers who had no regular place to meet. And some women are just as hedonistic as men. Jimmy's was trying to tap into that market.

So the following Sunday, Ricardo drove his rental car over to Buffalo and went to Jimmy's. Now, let me describe Jimmy's for you. The building that Jimmy's was in used to be a small three story warehouse, and originally, as I mentioned, it was in an industrial zone in Buffalo where all the buildings around it were also warehouses or small factories. But over the decades, as the neighborhood became gentrified, all the other warehouses were torn down and homes went up. So, Jimmy, in an effort to adapt and remain low-profile, had the outside of the warehouse remodeled to look like a house. It fit in with all the other houses on the street. If you drove by it, you'd never notice it. Like most gay bathhouses, it didn't have a name on the outside, or a red light like the old whorehouses. It just had a house number, just like all the other houses nearby. But if you were gay, you knew that number. And Jimmy was clever—when he had the outside redone, he made sure it was done to look a bit older. It didn't look like a brand new house—it looked like it had been there for years. Now, inside was a different story altogether. He spared no expense to have the most modern up-to-date amenities for his gay clients. There were three stories of everything you could want in a gay bathhouse. First of all, the security was good. When you checked in, you put all your valuables in a lockbox at the front desk, and you had the only key. Your entrance fee got you a clean towel and sandals. You could rent either a locker or a room to change out of your clothes, and of course both the lockers and the room had locks. And when it came to the rooms, you had quite a choice. You could rent a simple room with just a bed and some wall hooks to hang your clothes; or you could get a room with a king bed and a large flat screen TV with twenty different channels of porn; or you could get a room with a glory hole that opened up into one of the mazes, or to a room next door; or you could get a room with a sling. Lots of choices. On the first floor were the showers, the steam room, a Turkish dry-heat room, and a huge jacuzzi that would hold ten to twelve people. The lockers and rooms were all on the second and third floors, which also housed a maze, several dark rooms, and two B&D rooms with tie-down beds and some iron crosses with ropes and whips. There was also a large TV room with couches for group play. That TV room had three walls of 45-inch flat screens with porn showing all the time. There was a full staff of janitors who kept the place clean, and there were bins of free condoms and lubricant located throughout the building. It was the perfect gay bathhouse, which is why it was so popular. When the AIDS epidemic hit in the eighties, Jimmy's took a proactive position, and had the local health department come in every Friday and Saturday night for free HIV testing. Plus, there were rules posted everywhere, mandating safe sex. Yes, Jimmy's was a good place to be if you were gay or bisexual.

But, like I was saying, the market was changing. The internet, which had made Jimmy's so popular in the nineties as well as the first decade of the 2000s, was now providing apps like Grindr and Manlove where younger gays could just swipe one finger across their cell phone screen and be having sex with a nearby stranger within a few minutes. They didn't need to drive thirty or forty or a hundred miles to go to Jimmy's, and they didn't need to pay Jimmy's admission fee. The older clientele still came to Jimmy's, of course; but he was losing the market of the younger gay men. And every gay business depends on that steady influx of handsome young gay men with disposable cash to spend. So, as I said, Jimmy's had to adapt to the changing times. Buffalo, New York, like most other U.S. cities, had a large underground group of swingers and polyamorous couples. And Jimmy's was trying to appeal to them with its co-ed Sundays.

Ricardo was thinking about all of this as he drove over to Jimmy's that particular Sunday, a few days after he had visited Phillipe... And I suppose I should say a bit more about Ricardo's mood that day. I mentioned he had grown weary of life lately—but it was more than that. As I said, he was no longer a young man. There was a time, because of his looks, that he attracted a lot of lovers, both men and women. But no one really ages well, and the older one gets, the more the young lovers just evaporate. And you can say what you want about love, but the fact is, when it comes to sex, everyone prefers young lovers. Given a choice between a 30-year old and a 60-year old lover, which would you prefer? Yes, I thought so. And that was the boat that Ricardo was in. He was just too old to attract young lovers—male or female—anymore, and the reality of that had been settling in on him, or rather, closing in on him. Now, when I say "lovers", I am referring to relationships, affairs, ongoing things... you know, when you meet someone and there's that chemistry, and you end up seeing them again, and sooner or later, end up in bed... That's the kind of lover that had evaporated from Ricardo's life. Gay bathhouses are, of course, quite different. Age doesn't matter there because... well, because, it just doesn't. There's no relationship being sought there—it's just about sex. And basically, the gay baths and the brothels of Panama had been Ricardo's only form of sexual companionship for a few years now, and of the two, bathhouses were the most economical.

What? No, he hadn't given up on women... Well,

maybe he had a little... or maybe they had given up on him. You don't know how it is, because you are young; but Ricardo would go to some bar, or some event, and the women there wouldn't even notice him. You know how you can tell when you're being "vibed"—when some woman notices you, even when she pretends she doesn't, but you feel a certain energy from her? You know that feeling? Of course you do—you are young and handsome. Well, let me warn you, that experience does not continue in life as you get older. Ricardo hadn't experienced it in years. But that is exactly what intrigued him about the co-ed Sundays at Jimmy's. There's a hierarchy to desire, you know. The best is when a lover who you love desires you; the second best is when a stranger just desires you for that moment for sex; and the third situation is when you pay for sex and the other person is willing to act like she or he desires you. Well, for Ricardo, women had only been in that third zone for several years. He was hoping that maybe at Jimmy's that Sunday, there might be a woman, even as part of a couple, who was in that second zone. There's nothing quite as thrilling as a woman who desires you, is there? Even if she's just there for a sexual romp, at least she's not acting... So that was Ricardo's mindset as he drove over to Jimmy's that day. He knew he was getting his hopes up, but he couldn't help it.

Anyway, as Ricardo approached Jimmy's, he saw that there were lots of cars parked on the block. A good sign, he thought; they must be busy. He ended up parking about three blocks away from the bathhouse. He parked, got out, locked his car, and started walking towards Jimmy's. It was a beautiful sunny afternoon, that particular Sunday, and Ricardo was enjoying the walk. But as he crossed the first intersection, he noticed a legless man in a wheelchair coming the opposite way. The man was Ricardo's age, which is to say, old, but his arms were sinewy, muscular and deeply tanned. But his face was gaunt, lined, toothless, and worn-out. The cut-off bottoms of his jeans flopped and dangled just below the knees where his legs used to be. He had a raggedy white beard, and long gray hair that stuck out from underneath the cap he was wearing. The cap had an American flag on it with the word "VET" embroidered underneath it. The man did not look at Ricardo as he wheeled by. He seemed determined to get somewhere in a hurry as he worked the wheels of his wheelchair. Ricardo stepped aside to let him pass and then continued on to Jimmy's.

He entered Jimmy's non-descript front door and climbed the three steps up to the entrance window, steps he remembered from years before, when he used to visit on a regular basis. He paid his money at the window, and the man behind the bullet-proof glass buzzed him in. Once inside, the man handed him a room key and a towel, and Ricardo made his way to the second floor and found his room.

The place was pretty much just as he remembered it. As he took off his clothes and hung them on the hook, he wondered what the odds were that he ever had had sex in this particular room before. He wrapped the towel around himself and headed downstairs to the showers.

As he made his way to the showers, he kept his eyes peeled for any couples, but he saw none. Various men, with towels wrapped around their middles or simply draped over a shoulder, floated silently up and down the hallways, cruising in the same timeless manner as they have always done at Jimmy's, or any other gay bathhouse, for that matter. Ricardo wondered if he would see any women there that day at all. He did notice as he made his way to the shower that most of the men were at least his age, or older, some much older.

That's the thing about gay bathhouses, you know. They are the last haven for old gay men. Men who would be totally ignored in gay bars, passed over on any gay dating site, invisible in the gay neighborhoods and cruising areas... well, they have no other option. If they have no longtime partner, older gay men simply have no other place to find sex except the gay bathhouse. It's always been that way, but it was just that Ricardo had never dwelled on it before, because obviously, he had always been younger before, and therefore he too had been guilty of simply not seeing the old men that cruised the bathhouse unless they were particularly well-endowed. That's what everyone looks at in a bathhouse, you know—the size of the other man's package. But now Ricardo was the same age as these older men... So the reality of his age and his situation was quite obvious. He was in the same boat as all these other older guys. But I digress. Where was I? Oh, yes... so Ricardo showered, making sure to wash everywhere. One of the rules of etiquette in a gay bathhouse, you know, is that if you are going to present your body for others to touch or taste, then you should wash yourself carefully, and remove all body odor and all the dust, grime, and oil from the outside world. The bathhouse, as the name implies, is a very clean place, and it is considered a sin to not be clean and clean-smelling.

After showering, Ricardo walked around more, looking for women or couples. He walked back upstairs all the way to the third floor and worked his way down. He looked in the video room, the bondage room, the darkrooms; he walked past the rows of rooms, some of which had their doors open. As all the parked cars outside had indicated, the place was busy. But it was full of men. There were men in the video room, sitting together stroking each other while staring blankly at the porn movies on the large flat screens on the wall. One man was down on his knees performing oral sex on another man who was also transfixed by the porn on the wall. Ricardo walked into an S&M room but there was just one man there, lying in a leather sling, legs high and wide apart, waiting for someone to come in and fuck him. Ricardo walked past the rooms, slowing down to look into any room with an open door. But they all contained men, lying naked on the bed, stroking themselves, waiting for someone to come in and finish the job. He walked back down to the first floor and took a peek in the steam room and then into the Turkish dry heat room. Both had men sitting in the dark corners. But no females. So much for co-ed Sundays, he thought to himself. Then he remembered that Jimmy's had a small enclosed outdoor patio where people could sun themselves naked when the weather was nice. So he walked down the hallway to the door that led to the patio.

It was a bright day, that day in Buffalo, and stepping out into the sunlight on the enclosed patio from the dark hallways hurt Ricardo's eyes. He squinted and took a seat in the nearest lounge chair. The plastic webbing was hot, so he spread his towel over it and stretched out. It took his eyes several minutes to adjust to the bright light. He looked around and realized he was the only person out on the patio. Well, that's okay, he thought. It was a pleasant day. The patio was surrounded by a 12-foot high fence so it was perfectly safe to sunbathe naked there, and it was a pretty patio, surrounded by carefully maintained plants and shrubs along the fence. Ricardo thought he would just lay there for a few minutes and re-prioritize his agenda, since there were no women there.

It was at that moment that it dawned on Ricardo that his whole tour of Jimmy's for the past fifteen minutes had been solely to spot any women. How ironic, he thought to himself. There he was, cruising a gay bathhouse for women. This was a place he had frequented for years, albeit years ago, but a place where his sole purpose during all those years had been the pursuit of other men, and it amazed him how quickly his focus had shifted.

He lay there and thought about this for a bit, wondering why it was. Maybe he missed women more than he had realized. Or maybe he just wanted something new and different and had thought that a threesome would help him shake that despair that had enveloped him for so many weeks. After all, he thought, he wouldn't have made the drive to Buffalo that day if Phillipe hadn't told him about co-ed Sundays. No, there was something about the chance of connecting with a female body, albeit in a threesome or a group, that had enticed him to Jimmy's that day. It made him sad to think about this. He thought back to the last time he had been in a relationship with a woman. Not just one of the prostitutes he visited in the brothels of Panama, but an actual relationship... and he realized it had been more than a few years. And the weight of all that time seemed to make his body feel even older, heavier, as he lay there in the lounge chair.

But then he heard the door to the patio open, and voices coming from behind him. The chair he was lying on was close to the door, and he squinted to see three naked people walk past him and select lounge chairs just a few feet away. Because they all had their backs to him as they walked to the lounge chairs, it took Ricardo a minute or two to realize that one of the three people was a woman, a short and rather overweight woman, and it became clear relatively quickly that she was with the short overweight man, and they were talking to the third man, who was younger and slimmer. The short fat man was referring to the woman as his wife, and it became clear from the conversation that they had just met the younger man. The husband was saying to the younger man, "Well, my wife and I don't come here all that often, maybe once a month... and it's hit or miss... Sometimes there are six or seven other couples, and other times, it's just us."

And the younger man replied, "Well, my brother is inside, waiting on his friend. His friend is going to bring his wife. They've been here once before, I think he said. I've never met her, but my brother told me that she might try triple penetration today."

"Well, that'll be interesting," the husband replied.

The three people were spreading their towels out over the lounge chairs. They had discovered what Ricardo had discovered earlier—that the plastic webbing of the lounge chairs had gotten hot in the sun.

"I'm going in to get another towel," the fat woman said, and turned to walk inside.

"Don't do anything I wouldn't do," quipped the husband as she walked back past Ricardo to the patio door.

"Well, that leaves it wide open," said the younger man.

Ricardo watched the woman walk by him. She looked slightly Asian, maybe Polynesian, he couldn't be sure, but her skin was just a shade darker and her small eyes were sunk deep in the roundness of her face. Her large breasts hung low, over rolls of belly fat. Her large dark nipples were almost pointing straight down. Ricardo couldn't see her pussy because it was hidden by the large abdomen that hung down. She was not an attractive woman. Ricardo guessed her age was close to fifty—it was hard to tell. But youth, slenderness, and grace of movement were long since in her past.

The husband and the younger man continued to talk.

"Even if there're other couples here," the husband was saying, "we don't always play. Mostly we come for the lifestyle, just to be able to sunbathe naked and steam and relax."

"Yeah, I understand," the younger man replied. "It's nice to just hang out."

Ricardo, of course, didn't believe either one of them. The husband was eyeing the younger man, and the younger man was playing with himself and eyeing Ricardo at the same time that each were claiming that they were not there for sex. It's an almost universal phenomenon, you know, that when people are wanting sex, the last thing they'll do is *acknowledge* that they're wanting sex. They'll talk about sex as if they were disinterested, but all the while everyone is scoping each other out. And it's almost always impossible to discern exactly what people are after. Did the husband bring his fat wife here so that he could have guilt-free sex with men while other people banged his wife? Was the younger man attempting to befriend the couple so that he could create some orgy later with this couple and the couple that his brother was waiting for inside? That is, if what the younger man was saying was even true—that there was some other couple on the way. That's another universal phenomenon, you know... lying. Ricardo took another peek at the two men stretched out on their respective lawn chairs. They each were continuing to chat with each other about banal things, but both were adjusting and stroking their cocks gently. The younger man's cock was almost erect, while the older married man, who had to reach around his belly fat to touch his cock, was only at half-mast. The husband continued to look at the younger man, and the younger man continued to glance over at Ricardo. The younger man was relatively handsome, but the situation seemed complicated to Ricardo, so Ricardo just closed his eyes and pretended to sleep. He thought about what the younger man had said about his brother being inside waiting for some couple where the woman wanted triple penetration... Did that mean that this man and his brother and some third guy were going to all fuck this woman at the same time? Ricardo thought about the math... what if the woman wanted two cocks in her pussy at the same time? Would one brother's cock be rubbing against the other brother's cock? It seemed rather incestuous to Ricardo, and not appealing... Anonymous sex should definitely be anonymous—between strangers—that was the whole point—to be totally sexual without any complications, like knowing the other person.

Ricardo lay there in the sun with his eyes closed while the younger man and the husband continued to talk.

"I tried pegging for the first time last week," the younger man was saying.

"Oh," said the husband, "how did you like that?"

"I liked it... I may try it again."

Ricardo wondered if the younger man was trying to signal to the husband that he was willing to let the husband's wife use a dildo or strap-on on him. It seemed an absurd thing to mention at a gay bathhouse when there were so many real cocks around. But maybe that's why the younger man was befriending the couple.

"I'm going to see what Irma's up to," said the married man. He stood up, wrapped his towel around himself and walked inside. She had been gone for a bit, Ricardo thought, longer than it would take to grab another towel from the front desk.

Ricardo kept his eyes closed as the husband walked past him, still pretending to be asleep. Then he slowly opened one eye just the tiniest bit, just a slit, and looked through his eyelashes at the younger man. The younger man was stroking himself more rapidly now; he was fully erect; and staring at Ricardo's body. Ricardo didn't mind what the man was doing, but he intuited that there was a good probability that the man would get up soon and approach him and try to initiate sex, which at this point Ricardo didn't want, at least not with this man. So Ricardo rolled over onto his side, turning his head away from the man. He pretended to wake up, then sat up slowly, grabbed his towel and walked back into the bathhouse without looking back.

But coming in from the bright sunlight of the patio into the darkness left Ricardo temporarily blind. He needed a few minutes for his eyes to adjust, so he hugged the wall and moved very slowly down the hallway, towards the hissing sound of the steam room. The door to the steam room was illuminated by a soft overhead light. Ricardo felt for the door handle, found it, and stepped inside. He eased his way past several men sitting together on the large tiled sitting steps until he found an empty space away from them, spread his towel out, and sat down on one half of his towel, then draped the other half of the towel over his lap.

You do know those various codes of steam room communication, don't you? That if one covers themselves in the steam room, they want to be left alone? But if they sit naked exposing themselves, it means that they might be open to playing with the right person? And if they sit there and play with themselves, it means they are open to being fondled by anyone who passes by? Yes, I thought so. My instinct about you was right—you are someone who's been around. First time in Belgium? Ah, yes, I thought not.

Anyway, Ricardo had gone out to the patio to figure

out what he was going to do, but had been interrupted by those three people. So he figured he would sit quietly in the steam room to think in private. Clearly, whatever fantasy he had been having that there might be a gaggle of attractive swingers or voluptuous women cruising the bathhouse looking for someone like him to join them... well, that fantasy was total nonsense, he realized. Not that there aren't lots of attractive swingers in the world. But they weren't at Jimmy's that day, and they weren't going to be in Ricardo's life, that day or ever again. That's how he felt, at any rate.

So he sat there quietly in the dark, thinking. Somehow coming to Jimmy's that day had just made his depression worse. But he realized that it was because he had gotten his hopes up—that's why he was feeling worse. He had gotten his hopes up about women.

You know the myth about Pandora, don't you? How Pandora opened the sealed box that Zeus had forbidden her to open, and released all the evils of the world? And the story goes that the last thing to fly out of the box was hope, and the usual interpretation given to that myth is that Zeus gave the world hope in order to keep them going when they were being plagued by the evils of the world. Well, of course, that's the wrong interpretation. Hope was the last thing to fly out of the box because hope is the worst evil of all. It's the hope that things will get better that always leads to the biggest disappointments. Well, that's what had happened to Ricardo that day. He had let himself hope that he would be having wild uninhibited sex with beautiful women that day and, of course, that simply wasn't going to happen. And what made Ricardo feel worse was that he had done it all to himself. Phillipe hadn't led him on about co-ed Sundays—she had just mentioned that it existed. No, it was Ricardo's own stupid hope that had enticed him to drive all the way to Buffalo; his own stupid hope for contact with female flesh that had filled his head with images; his own stupid hope for something external to himself, some type of female deus ex machina to reach out and save him.

Ricardo sat there in the steam room and just shook his head. That's the problem with depression, you know—it's hard to think your way out of it—and Ricardo's thoughts were spiraling downwards. He kept thinking that he was just another old lonely bisexual man, just like all the other old lonely bi or gay men there in the bathhouse that day, all just groping their way in the dark, hoping to find a little bit of naked flesh to kiss or fuck.

And so, because he was feeling so bad, Ricardo decided that he had had enough of Jimmy's; that he would simply get dressed and go back to his hotel and drink. So he stood up and began to make his way out of the steam room. As he got to the door, one of the men sitting on the tile steps reached up and ran his hand over the front of Ricardo's towel and said, "Leaving so soon?" Ricardo looked at the man. He was not unhandsome. The man was stroking himself and had a nice erection. But Ricardo was simply not in the mood for gay sex that day. Sex is almost always a mood thing, you know, and Ricardo was too absorbed, or too despondent, or too depressed for sex now. So he just shook his head no to the man, and stepped out of the steam room. He took a quick rinse shower, and walked slowly up to the second floor to his room. But in order to get to his room, he had to walk by one of the S&M rooms, and he noticed it was very crowded, so he paused in the doorway to see what was going on. He had to look over the shoulders of several men to get a view. Well, what he saw was that Irma, the wife from the patio, had hoisted herself up into a leather sling, and was lying on her back being fucked by someone who was standing in between her legs. Her husband was standing at the head of the sling, moving the sling, with Irma in it, back and forth. Irma's pudgy legs were splayed out and held aloft by the two separate leather leg rests of the sling, putting her pussy at the exact height whereby a man could just stand there and penetrate her, which was exactly what was going on. This man was just standing there, in between Irma's legs, and the movement of the sling back and forth by the husband, glided Irma's pussy back and forth over the man's erect cock. So, basically, Irma was fucking the man, and the other men standing there were waiting their turn to fuck Irma. Lying down, she didn't look quite as obese, but she was still fat. Her large breasts hung down to either side of her chest. Ricardo could see her pussy at last—there was only a small tuft of hair above the thin dark gaping lips, lips that were wrapped around that stranger's cock. Some other man approached Irma's face and positioned his cock near Irma's mouth. With each back-and-forth movement, she would lick at it as she passed by. Ricardo looked around the room at the faces of the men, all intently gazing at Irma or at the man fucking Irma. Everyone was stroking themselves waiting their turn.

The man fucking Irma tensed up, then reached down, pulled his cock out of Irma and ejaculated all over her fat stomach. There was a murmur of approval from the other men. The man gave his cock a few strokes to squeeze the last drops of cum out of it, then stepped aside. The next man in line stepped in and slid his erect cock into Irma and the fucking started again.

Ricardo stepped out of the S&M room and walked down the hall, shaking his head. What he had seen made no sense to him. This was a gay bathhouse, yet here were all these men standing in line to fuck this woman, this obese unattractive woman. Was it solely because she had a pussy? Were they gay but curious what pussy felt like? Were they straight but only came to the bathhouse to participate in a gangbang? Were they all stupid not to be wearing condoms? Ricardo, as you know, had always been an advocate of sexual freedom, and saw nothing wrong with anonymous sex, but this was not some joyous orgy... In fact, it was about the most grim group sex he had ever seen.

He walked back to his room, went inside, locked the door, stretched out on his bed and just stared at the ceiling.

He had hoped that coming to the states would shake his malaise. But like that old saying about the only zen you find at the top of the mountain is the zen you brought with you... well, Ricardo had brought his malaise and his depression with him from Panama. Still, he thought, maybe it was just bad luck, or bad timing. Not every day can be an orgy, he told himself. He had just come to Jimmy's on a bad day. He still had a trip to Europe scheduled; he could still visit Spain; he still had a few friends, maybe, in Menorca from his youth; and he was flying into Amsterdam, the sex capital of the world; and he could still go to the sex clubs in Berlin and maybe find the type of male-female group sex that evidently wasn't going to happen at Jimmy's. That's the problem with the U.S., he thought: all talk and no action. If a Berlin club promised sex, there was going to be sex. If a U.S. club promised sex, there was just going to be the promise. Well, he was an idiot for letting himself get tricked again, he thought. But okay, he would deal with it. He would move on. He got up and put his clothes on and got ready to leave Jimmy's. It wasn't the first time he had gone to a gay bathhouse and not had sex, he told himself. He could deal with it.

He walked down the stairs, tossed his towel in the dirty towel hamper at the front desk and handed in his sandals, got his valuables out of the lockbox, and stepped outside.

It was now late afternoon, and still warm and sunny in Buffalo. Ricardo walked back to his car, not really looking at anything, but aware of the slight breeze in the air, and the sounds of a suburban neighborhood all around him. Cars were going by, taking people wherever they were going. Pots were banging in the houses that he passed. Things were happening. People were going on with their lives all around him. There in suburbia New York, he felt like a stranger in a strange land, just a temporary visitor, disguised as a human being, walking back to his car.

He heard the yelling first, then looked up to see that same legless man in the wheelchair about a block away, wheeling his way towards him again. How strange, Ricardo thought, to be passing him again in the street. But this time the man was yelling, yelling at no one in particular.

"Jesus is coming! Jesus is coming!" The man seemed to be yelling. *Oh dear*, Ricardo thought, *he's crazy*. The man was wheeling his chair at a furious pace, coming towards Ricardo. He bounced off the curb and crossed the intersection. Ricardo stepped aside as he had done previously to let him pass, but this time he gave the man a wider berth than before. But the man stopped in front of Ricardo and made eye contact with him. Except that it wasn't eye contact. There was nothing in this man's eyes but a wild look.

"Have you been saved?" the legless man shouted at Ricardo.

Ricardo took a step back.

"Be washed in the blood and rise like Jesus!" the man shouted.

Ricardo opened his mouth, but thought better of it. He looked to his left to make his escape.

"Be washed in the blood and rise like Jesus in three days!" the man repeated.

Ricardo took three steps to his left and left the legless man facing the other direction. The man started laughing. "All dead! All dead except those washed in blood."

Ricardo walked quickly to his car, glancing over his shoulder to make sure the legless man was wheeling his chair in the opposite direction.

Crazy Vietnam vet, he thought to himself, as he reached his rental car and climbed in. *Fucked up men, fucked up vets*. He started the car and drove back to Hamburg.

When he got to Hamburg, he stopped at a convenience store near the hotel and brought two bottles of wine: one for that night, and one more in case the first didn't do the trick. And as he was walking through the hotel lobby with his wine, he noticed that there was some kind of event happening in the ballroom off the main lobby—it had a sign up in front saying it was closed for a private party. He paused to read the sign, and saw that it was a wedding reception. The door to the ballroom was slightly ajar and Ricardo could have looked inside, but he didn't. But he could hear people talking and laughing and having a good time. And of course that just made him more depressed, and so took his two bottles up to his room and drank them both until he passed out on the bed.

Well, I see the hour is late and I have not answered your question. But, if you are still interested, meet me here tomorrow and I will finish my story. You know, this bar serves dinner between five and seven in the evening. Nothing fancy, but very adequate. If you have time, I will invite you to be my guest for dinner. What do you say? Yes, good. Well, meet me here at five tomorrow, and we will dine and I will tell you the rest of the story.

Chapter 3: Passport

Ah there you are, right on time. Good to see you again. Yes well, sit down, yes, here's the menu. I took the liberty of ordering a bottle of wine. Would you like a glass? Yes, it's quite a nice wine. No, no take your time with the menu, we have all evening... well at least I do... order whatever you like.

What? No, no, no, I didn't mean to suggest last night that Ricardo wasn't happy. But it's just that... well, the word happy is just such a useless word when it comes to men, isn't it? I mean, if you had asked him, he would have said he was happy with life, but by that he would have meant that he was grateful. After all, he was alive, and he was doing exactly what he wanted in life. He had always wanted to be a writer, and there he was, living in a beautiful foreign country, and making a living as a writer. He was... how do you Americans put it? He was living the dream. But happy is not a good word for men, because no man is really happy. I remember one conversation I had with him once when he was explaining to me that he thought men are just drones... No, no, male bee drones, not those flying robot machines... He actually believed that men are like the bee drones whose only purpose was to service the queen bee. Even though he was bisexual and had lots of sex with men, he really thought that the sole evolutionary function of man—what their bodies had evolved for—was just to produce seed to impregnate women, and that when we can no longer put out, so to speak, that life would just sweep us out of the nest to die. It's funny—many other male writers also seem to have held that opinion. Did you know that Hemingway thought that every man was assigned a certain number of orgasms, and that when a man reached his last orgasm, he would die? It's true. Now, Ricardo didn't share Hemingway's view, but he did believe that we were just on this earth to have sex... and that sex and death were inextricably linked. Do you know what the French slang for orgasm is? La petite mort—the little death. Yes, he liked that phrase, too. He always felt that the act of sex was both his sole purpose but at the same time was an affirmation of his mortality.

No, no he had no children. Yes, I know, it's ironic. In some ways his psychological make-up was out of sync with his physical needs and proclivities. He loved women; he loved having sex with them; but he didn't seem to be able to sustain a relationship for any length of time. I suppose many writers are like that... maybe that's what makes them writers.

Ah, here's the waiter. Order whatever you'd like. It's my treat. I rarely meet someone who is as taken by Ricardo's books as I have been. Yes, that's an excellent choice. Well, for me... hmmm, ah well... *Monsieur, je vais avoir l'habitude. Oui, merci.*

Yes, I eat here often, it's true. I'm a creature of habit, I guess... and certain habits I share with Ricardo, I guess. But anyway, where was I? Let's see... I told you about Ricardo going to Jimmy's... and about him seeing that Irma woman getting gangbanged in the sling. Well, he told me that seeing those men line up to fuck that woman was just too depressing to watch. But when he first described it to me, I didn't understand why it had affected him so much. My first thought was that maybe he was struggling with the fact that he had gotten older, and was realizing that the type of anonymous sex that had always been so liberating for him when he was young was now just an empty trap, because it was all that was left for him. He had eschewed long-term relationships and commitments for the pleasures of sex, and now he had to reap that harvest. But I discarded that theory because I realized he had always enjoyed those types of sexual relationships... Then, I wondered if maybe he had gotten depressed because maybe he saw a bit of himself in Irma. But I discarded that theory, too. I just didn't know what to think at first.

But anyway, back at the hotel that night, as I think I mentioned, he drank rather heavily, and then late into the evening he passed out on the bed, still dressed in his clothes, and he had this strange dream. He dreamed he was standing on the banks of a great river, a vast river whose width must have been twenty miles or more. The water was gray, a dirty green-gray, and the sky had low heavy gray clouds that stretched across the entire vista. Far beyond the river, Ricardo could see a distant shore, whose outlines were blurred by the mist, clouds, and distance. He looked left and right. He could see no people, no towns, no signs of civilization. Then he looked closely at the river. It wasn't just water. It was full of objects: old refrigerators, cars, timbers, barrels, steel containers. It was as if a huge tsunami had swept away an entire city. Ricardo looked closer. The river was also filled with dead bodies, bloated, blackened, bobbing up and down between all the huge metal objects that dwarfed the bodies. A horrible revulsion went through him. He turned around and began to run away as fast as he could.

What? Well, no, that's an interesting question. Let me think about it for a minute... Yes, it's true that all the happenings in U.S. politics were going on at this same time, and yes, Ricardo was aware of them. Even expats in Panama get all the U.S. news online. But no, I don't think that was *directly* affecting his mind. It's true, he had very little faith in people as a group. He could be very loyal to his friends but he was convinced that the human race was doomed, and therefore politics, or any effort to organize or save humanity was, in his opinion, futile... Well, no... he was more cynical than even that. He pretty much hated all politics. But even though the U.S. political system was imploding at that time, Ricardo really had removed himself from all of that a decade earlier when he moved to Panama. Now... of course, that said, you know... Carl Jung did have that theory of the collective unconscious... and whether the implosion of American politics was a synchronistic reflection of Ricardo's state of mind or vice versa, I can't say—I'm no Jungian. But my opinion is that no, that the state of U.S. politics was not a factor in Ricardo's state of mind.

So anyway, a few weeks later, Phillipe called to tell Ricardo that his new passport had arrived. Ricardo was very glad to hear this. His flight to Europe was only a week or so away and he was getting nervous about not having his passport in time. He renewed his driver's license in Hamburg, and then went to New York City and had concluded all his business with his publisher, his lawyer, and his tax accountant. He had paid his taxes, reviewed his royalty payments, and signed a new contract for another two books... all the things that were remaining on his checklist of items that he had returned to the states to do. Now all he needed to do was to pick up his passport and take that trip to Spain. He told Phillipe he'd drive up to Hamburg the next evening and suggested that they have dinner together.

"Ooooh! Dinner out?" exclaimed Phillipe. "Like, at a restaurant?"

"Well, of course at a restaurant Phillipe—I'm not going to grill hot dogs over a fire in the park," laughed Ricardo.

"What shall I wear? Are we going somewhere nice?"

"Jesus Christ, Phillipe," said Ricardo. "Look, I'm wearing jeans. You pick where you want to go, and you dress however you want. I'll pick you up at seven, okay?"

"Oooh, I love it when you get dominant," teased Phillipe. "Okay, see you at seven."

So the next evening, Ricardo picked Phillipe up, and she handed him the special delivery envelope that contained his passport, and they drove to Lola's, a tiny Italian restaurant in Hamburg. Lola's was considered a proper upscale restaurant for Hamburg, but only a few people, which included Phillipe and Ricardo, knew that the owners were two lesbians named Lois and Charlene. Lois and Charlene never mingled with the guests at the restaurant, but they kept close control over the quality of the food and the service, and the restaurant had a good following.

"How did you get reservations?" Ricardo asked as he parked the car.

"Oh, well, you know me," Phillipe smiled. "And I know everyone."

"Yes," Ricardo laughed. He turned off the car's engine, but took a moment to open the envelope and look at his passport. The cover was all shiny and stiff.

"Oh, let me see the photo!" Phillipe exclaimed.

Ricardo opened it to the photo page, looked and winced. "Oh! It's horrible," he said, and quickly closed the passport and shoved it in his shirt pocket. "Come on, let's eat," he said, and got out of the car.

Inside, the maitre d' nodded at Phillipe and seated them at a table right away. Phillipe was wearing a tight fitting Ann Taylor dress. *She's totally passable,* Ricardo thought to himself as he watched her walk in front of him. The maitre d' pulled her chair back and Phillipe sat down with a flourish. Ricardo noticed a man at a nearby table give her an approving once-over. Ricardo sat down, shook his head and smiled.

"You do make a nice entrance, Phillipe," he said.

"Years of practice," Phillipe said and smiled.

A waiter came by with menus and told them of the specials. Ricardo ordered a glass of wine and Phillipe ordered a Campari and soda with a twist of lemon.

As Ricardo was studying the menu, Phillipe asked: "You didn't like your passport photo?"

"No... well, no. The photo was accurate. I'm just getting older, and I don't like that."

"Where did you have it taken?"

"At the Walmart near the mall."

"Ah," said Phillipe. "Well, of course. I had mine done at Wally's Camera downtown." She leaned forward, and said in a whisper, "They'll airbrush it if you ask them to. My photo came out fabulous!"

Ricardo looked at Phillipe and said, "Do you know what the most common use of a passport photo in Panama is?"

"No, darling, what?"

"To identify a body."

"Well, that's gruesome. But at least I can show my friends my passport, and you can't."

"Touché," admitted Ricardo, and returned to studying the menu.

"Are you excited about your trip?" Phillipe asked.

"Hmmm. Yes... and no... I still haven't decided exactly on where I'm going."

"Well, Spain of course," said Phillipe.

"Yes, but, I'm flying into Amsterdam. I thought I

might spend a few days there first... you know, see the sights... before flying on to Spain..."

"Oh, yes, the *sights*," said Phillipe. "Tell me what *sights* you might be interested in seeing in Amsterdam."

"Well, there's the Van Gogh museum..."

"Oh *please!*" interrupted Phillipe, "you know what I mean."

Ricardo sighed, pursed his lips, then said, "Well, before I answer that, let me tell you about Jimmy's."

"Oh! You went? Yes, please! Do tell," exclaimed Phillipe.

So Ricardo told Phillipe about his experience at Jimmy's and about how it left him feeling, and Phillipe listened attentively. Despite all her affectations, she did genuinely care about Ricardo, you know.

"Anyway," Ricardo was finishing up, "there was something about that line of men, just lining up to fuck that fat woman, one after the other, all without condoms, all with a kind of a blank look on their faces... I don't know... it left me feeling so depressed, so... so anti-sex... so... like, what's the point of it all? You know? I mean, it really made me question a lot of what I do. I don't mean to be gross, but those guys would have fucked any hole... not that fucking is always about fucking someone attractive, but they would have lined up to fuck anything... and the thing that really freaked me out, Phillipe... the thing that really got to me, is that for a brief moment, I considered getting in line with them... that's what really bothered me... that on some level, I was just like them."

Phillipe was quiet, just nodding her head and looking serious, and then finally she said, "Well, in the first place, Ricky-boy, you didn't get in line with them... and in the second place, physical beauty *does* make a difference... and in the third place, sex is always about surrendering, about giving in. And the interplay of these three dynamics is what makes things interesting. There's always this conflict between giving in to physical beauty and the carnality of just animal fucking. It's not resolvable, you know that."

She paused, still looking serious, then said: "You know, Ricky-boy, in my world, beauty is everything. There is nothing sadder than an ugly transsexual. I hate to say that because everyone has their struggle, but in this world, beauty is everything, and I don't just mean the modern world—it's always been that way. Beauty rules. I spend hours a day making sure I look beautiful. Why? Because time is my enemy. You are lucky. Men can just age and still look good. Not so for women. I have to keep my estrogen shots on a rigorous schedule. I know that my status in this world, especially in my circle, is based on beauty and bravado. They're quite interchangeable, you know. But seriously, Ricardo, you just got freaked out watching a bunch of bisexual men go hog wild getting to fuck some old dumb cow. You didn't fuck her. But that doesn't mean you shouldn't let yourself go with some beautiful person who invites you in. You can't give up on sex just because the sight of some people fucking is ugly. There are certain sex acts, you know, good sex acts, really good sex acts, that really do need to be done behind closed doors with no one watching."

Ricardo gave a short laugh, but then said, "Yeah, I know, but somehow it still bothers me... I don't know... Maybe this is just what happens when people get old."

"No! I reject that, Ricky-boy. Look, sex is sex, passion is passion no matter what the age. You're confusing availability with reliability. Look... you like wine, right?"

"You know I do."

"You like good wine, yes?"

"Of course."

"If a waiter brought you cheap crappy wine and told you it was free, all you could drink for free, or... that you could have a twelve-dollar glass of a very good wine, which would you choose?"

"I would choose the good wine, of course."

"And you wouldn't mind spending the twelve dollars even when you could have the crappy wine for free?"

"No, of course not. Twelve dollars is not unreasonable for a glass of very good wine."

"But if you were on a deserted island, and the only wine that was available was crappy wine, you might have a glass or two."

"Yeah."

"Exactly... You know why there are so many crappy cheap wines on the market? Because people, the masses of people, will buy them. They're available. Marketing has made people think that crappy wine is good wine, but you and I know the truth. We know to be selective. Well, sex is no different. The bathhouses are just the Walmarts of sex. There's lot of choices there, and the variety of choices is very stimulating—it's exciting to see all the choices—but it's mostly crappy sex there, occasionally some good bargains, but mostly lousy crappy sex. And just like with wine, you don't give up tasting good wine just because you happen to get some bad wine. You were hoping to taste some fine wine at Jimmy's but all that was there was cheap white-trash bathtub wine... Butall that means is that you should redouble your efforts to find some really good wine. And, lucky you! You will have the chance to sample some rare European vintages... Ha, yes, Ricky-boy, you need to throw yourself back into the fray, and go down to the cellars and look for the good rare wines. Europe, yes, I'm glad you're going there. It will be so good for you. The

U.S. really has no clue about sex, you know. I think it is fate that is sending you to Amsterdam first—and you should listen to fate. Indulge yourself there, really let yourself go. Do it all. That's my advice."

"And how is that different from those guys at Jimmy's, lining up to fuck that woman?" asked Ricardo.

Phillipe laughed and said, "It's the difference between good wine and crappy wine, my friend; the difference between great sex with beautiful people and crappy sex with ugly people; the difference between enjoying life and enduring it. Life isn't fair, Ricky-boy; some people get more, and you, my friend, are one of those people. You can afford a good glass of wine; you can afford to go to Europe; you can afford to spend a few days in Amsterdam; so take advantage of it. Don't just count your blessings—seize them and squeeze the juice out of them. Let that experience at Jimmy's be a lesson in what to avoid. Go hang out with beautiful European people and get some great sex. Fuck Jimmy's."

Ricardo laughed and said, "Yeah, Jimmy's was a real downer."

"That's right!" Phillipe said. "Put it behind you! Take a page from my book. People don't need bravery— they need bravado. You need to go to Europe and get some good sex. Now, let's order some food. I'm starving."

And so for the second time in Ricardo's trip to the U.S., Phillipe had said some words that would later make an impact on Ricardo, although maybe not in the way that Phillipe had intended when she said them to Ricardo that night over dinner... Ah, speaking of dinner, here's our food. It looks delicious. Here, let me refill your glass. À la vôtre!

Chapter 4: Decision

Ah, yes. Mine is delicious—how's yours? Good. So where was I? Oh, yes. So Ricardo's flight to Amsterdam was not scheduled to leave for another week or so after his dinner with Phillipe, so Ricardo had that time to kill. That's the problem with airline travel nowadays—you have to book in advance to get a good price, but then you're stuck with that date. If you want to change your flight to an earlier day, the airlines charge you two to three hundred dollars! I know you won't believe this because you are young, but there was a time when the prices for flights were all the same, no matter what day you bought tickets for. And you could just drive to the airport, buy a ticket and hop on a plane. You smile, but it's true. Of course, that was years ago... decades ago, really... So anyway, Ricardo just had to wait. He was just glad his passport had arrived in time, and so he figured he would just wait the week. Normally, waiting was something that never bothered him. He was used to it. He had a lot of practice at waiting, because he was a writer, and so he would normally just take his little laptop to some coffee shop and sit and drink coffee and write. He once told me that he thought seventy-five percent of life was just sitting around and waiting. He said he got some of his best writing done when he was just stuck somewhere for days waiting for a train or plane or bus to take him somewhere else.

He always said that writing kept him sane, but I suspect what he really meant was that writing kept him from going mad. That's the thing about this world, you know... look at it long enough and you realize that it really *is* insane.

As children, we learn about cause and effect. But if you're a writer, or an artist, and you look at this world, well... you quickly see that there is no cause and effect. Things just happen... bad things... and then afterwards, as we pick up the pieces, we rationalize it. We say, *well, this was caused by such and such.* And even if good things happen, we analyze it as if *we* had something to do with it. We tell ourselves, well I studied hard and worked hard and then life rewarded me with a good job... or some such nonsense. No... things just happen. It's all random. Look at life long enough and you realize, it's all just random.

But anyway... as I was saying... normally, Ricardo was able to keep all this madness at bay because of his writing, but this time, stuck in a hotel in upstate New York for a week, somehow it was different. He would go to some coffee shop, open up his laptop, set up a blank page and try and write... but nothing came... Or rather, words would come and he'd type them, but then he'd look at what he had written, and just delete the page and start again. This went on for hours every day. That's the thing about writing, you know. It always brings you to exactly where you are at. And where Ricardo was at... was... nowhere. Normally the words flowed out of him and described all the weird and wild things that were either actually occurring to him or were based on things that were occurring around him in his life... Some of his books are quite funny, you know... But that particular week, he had nothing... nothing except a vast emptiness inside of him, an emptiness that had been building for months. He would sit there in a coffee shop and just stare at his computer screen... write, then delete, write more, delete it all, and just continue to stare at the empty screen. He would try moving to different coffee shops, or bars, or going back to his hotel. Nothing seemed to work. And nothing was working on paper because nothing was working inside of him, you see. He was beginning to realize how truly despondent he was.

He had simply assumed that he had just gotten weary while he was in Panama, and that it would pass, or that the scene at Jimmy's was depressing, but it would pass, but now he realized he was actually despairing. That's the funny thing about realizing something, you know. It's not that you suddenly get a new piece of information that gives you a new understanding... no, no... the pieces are always there, but suddenly they add up. The day when Ricardo realized he was in real despair was about the fourth day into his week of waiting. He was sitting at another coffee shop, trying to write, and somehow his mind was drifting back through the past few years. He wasn't trying to think of anything in particular—it was more like his mind was just *not thinking*— not focusing on anything. There were some customers sitting around him. He could hear the tinkling of coffee spoons, and the rustling of newspaper pages, or the clickety-click of other people typing on their laptops, or the sounds of people talking back in the kitchen, but the images that were coming up in his mind were all these faces, a collage of all the people he used to know, the friends he used to have, and how they had (for the most part) all died or had drifted away. But, of course it was really the fact that *he* had moved away from them. And he began to see his entire life as a tide going out, as him always slowly moving away from other people and, unlike the real tide that always comes back in, Ricardo's life was a wave that just kept moving out, retreating further out to sea, leaving this vast and empty beach behind him. And he just sat there feeling so sad, so despairing, so lonely. And it made no sense to him, you see... That's why it took him so long to see it... or rather, to *feel* it. Because it made no sense that he should be feeling so empty. His life was quite full. He was doing exactly what he wanted to do—living in Panama and writing books... and yet, he felt horrible. None of what he had accomplished seemed valuable to him—all of his published books, his lifestyle, his ability to come and go as he pleased... it all seemed pointless to him... he felt that he could die that day in that coffee shop, and no one would care because there was no one left to care... and this feeling worried him greatly... You know why?... Yes, that's exactly right, my friend. You are very astute. He *had* spent some time in rehab, and he didn't want to go down that path again. He knew he could control his drinking even if he was a little depressed, but not if he fell into that black hole of complete and utter abandoned despair. And it scared him. But there he was, feeling like he was standing on the edge of that horrible and bottomless abyss. So what did he do? Hmmm? What would you do? What would any of us do? Well, the truth is that everyone handles those existential crises differently. But Ricardo, well, he did the only thing he could think of—the only thing that had ever worked for him before. He made a conscious mental decision to throw himself into sex. That conversation with Phillipe kept coming back to him and he decided to take Phillipe's advice. Despite his experience at Jimmy's, he made this intellectual decision to try and get as much sex as he could. Phillipe had said that thing about fate offering him a way out of his despair, by arranging it that the cheapest flight was to Amsterdam, and Ricardo decided that he was going to take advantage of the trip and throw himself into sex when he got to Amsterdam... Now, I know that seems so counter-intuitive. If watching the anonymous mindless sex at Jimmy's had repulsed him, why would he decide to throw himself into anonymous mindless sex? Sort of reminds you of naturopaths, doesn't it? How they try and cure a disease by giving you potions that cause the very disease you're trying to get rid of? I mean, we don't cure alcoholism by giving a man more alcohol, do we? But here was Ricardo, deciding to deliberately pursue ignorant fuckery. And here was his logic: he recognized that his depression was really a deprivation—a sensory deprivation. He had few friends left and no intimate friends left. He hadn't had a girlfriend or boyfriend for years... He hadn't been in love for many years and certainly no one he knew of was in love with him. And the fact is, people need those relationships. We can get by for a while without them, but eventually we begin to starve. And Ricardo recognized that his depression was really starvation. He was starved for a real relationship. But real relationships are rare, and the older you get, the rarer they get. At Ricardo's age, his options were quite limited—he might never find real love again—and he was starving and he needed a transfusion. He saw sex as a necessary triage to bind him up while he waited for love.

We're all still like babies, you know. They need both love and physical touch. They need both or they die. If they get one or the other, they'll survive physically, but they die emotionally. Even baby monkeys will cling to a piece of cloth, anything soft, if they are deprived of love and touching. That's how Ricardo viewed it anyway. He was sitting there in that coffee shop, thinking about nothing, just letting the memories of the past few years bubble up, when it dawned on him that he hadn't felt love, hadn't been in a real love relationship, for almost five years. He had had flings, of course. He had spent many nights in the brothels of Panama or afternoons in the bathhouses, but those moments of physical contact were just tiding him over, and he hadn't had them in a while, either. So as he sat there, in that coffee shop that day, he realized how desperate his situation was, and that he needed to act.

So when I said that he did the only thing that had ever worked for him before, I meant that in the full irony of that sentence. Because the fact was, he was starved for *love*. Sex was just a sugary substitute. But like that tide that was forever moving out to sea, Ricardo had always moved away from love. He simply never could commit to love, and so... over the years, all his true loves had slipped through his fingers. And Ricardo saw the dilemma. What he needed was a real human relationship, but he simply had never been able to make that work, so he had always chosen sex. And so that was the only choice that was left open to him now. People really can't change you know, and Ricardo couldn't, either.

What? Oh, you think people can change? Really? Well, I don't want to dissuade you—you are young and change always seems possible when one is young. So maybe we can just agree to disagree. So let's just say that Ricardo felt that *he* couldn't change—that his life's patterns were too well formed, like links in a long chain. Now, I don't mean to imply to Ricardo had never loved—that's not what I'm talking about. He had certainly felt love, had certainly been in love. But making a love relationship work—making a marriage work, or any long-term relationship work—takes a certain patience, a certain continual sacrifice, a certain generosity... that Ricardo never had... But anyway, let's just say that at that moment, sitting there in that coffee shop in Hamburg, New York, staring at that image of his life receding away from him forever, for whatever psychological reason, Ricardo made a decision to do the one thing he knew how to do, to throw himself back into the skin trade. Now, you're probably thinking he was just repeating something that had never worked before—that isthe definition of neurosis isn't it? Repeating the same dysfunctional behaviors? But the reason we repeat them, is that they *do* work... maybe poorly, but on some level, they do work.

And one other thing that you have to know about Ricardo. He was a very determined fellow. Once he made up his mind to do something, he did it. Over a decade ago, against all the advice of his friends at the time, he quit his job and moved to Panama, and made that work. He wanted to be a writer, and he made that work. He wanted to live his life the way he wanted, and he did. And so, once he made his mind up that he was going to dive back into the realm of the senses, into pure carnality and flesh and pleasure, once he had decided that... that's exactly what he did.

So when I said last night that in order to understand what happened to Ricardo in Europe, why he was there, that you first had to understand his state of mind, this is what I meant—that he had this combination of feeling deep despair, being at the end of his rope, of being desperate, and then making up his mind to plunge headfirst into pure carnal pleasure, hoping that he could find his way back out. *That* was his state of mind....

So now... now let me tell you what happened in Europe.

Chapter 5: Amsterdam

This is such a good wine. Here, let me refill your glass. I don't know anything about this particular winery, but the vintage is Nero d'Avola. It's a varietal grown in Sicily, and I like it. The Belgians are proud of their wines, I know; but I prefer a more primitive taste. You can taste the warm sun and earthy roots in this wine... Anyway, there was something about that decision of Ricardo's—that desperate decision to throw himself back into sex—that helped him get through his last few days in New York. I knew a psychologist who once told me that in therapy, it doesn't matter much what decision a depressed patient makes—that it's the act of making a decision that empowers the person, even if the decision is not the best one in the world. Maybe that's true, I don't know. Ricardo's depression didn't lift, but he did find something to look forward to, and something to do rather than fruitlessly type on his computer. He was originally going to simply fly into Amsterdam and then catch the next flight to Barcelona, but instead, he decided to spend a few days in Amsterdam. So he booked a hotel online and started to think about what type of experience he wanted. Most people, you know, even those who think they're sophisticated about sex, well... they do what people have always done... which is to wait for sex to happen and then try and shape that partner into some experience that they secretly want. A guy secretly wants a dominant lover or maybe a very submissive lover, but he never lays that out when he meets someone—no, no, he waits until he's in bed with the person that he's met and wooed, and then he starts hinting or manipulating that person to try to turn them into the lover he wants. It's ridiculous. Well, Ricardo knew that if there was anywhere on earth that was a buffet table of different sexual experiences, it was Amsterdam. So he spent a lot of time thinking about what type of sexual experience he wanted.

Of course, the ironic thing is that no one knows what they actually want. It's the biggest irony of all, don't you think? What do I mean by that? Well, everyone thinks they know what they want, what will make them happy; everyone has an image in their mind about the person or the thing or the situation that will make them happy. The whole "free will" and "pursuit of happiness" ideology is based on this idea. But the fact is that we have no idea what makes us happy until we are actually happy, and most of the time, the thing that we think will make us happy actually makes us miserable. People spend their life pursuing something that they believe will bring them happiness, but if they finally get that thing, well, it turns out to be quite empty.

I remember a study done years ago where they asked some young people to describe their perfect partner, and everyone had a specific preference: tall and blonde, or brunette, or skinny redhead... whatever... and then they gave these same people free membership in a dating site and followed them for two years...and when those people met someone who they liked and started dating and starting forming a relationship and started being lovers, the scientists compared who these people had chosen versus what type they said they liked, and of course, there was no correlation. One guy might have said he liked tall blondes but then fell in love with a short brunette, or one woman might have said that she liked muscular athletic types but then fell in love with a computer nerd. But the interesting thing was that once these people were in a love relationship and the scientists asked them again to describe their ideal partner, the descriptions had totally morphed! The guy who said he liked tall blondes but ended up with a short brunette now claimed that his ideal partner was a short brunette, and the woman who originally said she liked muscular athletes but ended up with a skinny computer nerd now claimed her ideal mate was a bookwormish computer nerd. In other words, their experiences shaped their preferences, not the other way around. But then the scientists followed these subjects for another two years. Some of the couples had gotten married, but some of the other couples had broken up. And when the scientists asked those subjects who had broken up what type of person they thought would make them happy, they had all reverted to their original preference: the guy who originally said he liked tall blondes but who had fallen in love with a short brunette and had then claimed that he liked short brunettes...well within three months of breaking up, he claimed that his preferred type was now tall blondes. And it was true of all the subjects they followed: the ones who ended up finding someone who made them happy ended up with someone who didn't match their so-called ideal type; and the ones who said they were happy for a while but broke up went back to saying that their original ideal type would be their perfect mate. The scientists didn't know what to conclude from all this. But to me, the conclusion was obvious: people have no fucking clue what makes them happy no matter how much they claim they do. We somehow get these imprints on our brain of what we think we want... but it has nothing to do with happiness.

And so it was with Ricardo. He flew to Schiphol

Airport in the Netherlands, and then caught the train to downtown Amsterdam. He had booked a hotel in the red light district. After a day's rest to recover from jet lag, he went out in pursuit of his so-called ideal sexual partner.

Now, you've been to Amsterdam, right? Yes, I thought so. Despite your youth, I could tell you were a man of experience. So I don't have to describe to you how the red light district works, how the girls all showcase themselves in the tall windows on the winding streets for the men to select? How the men step inside, the curtain is drawn, and the sex happens on the narrow beds? No, I thought I didn't. I imagine you have your preferences, too... We all do... or at least we think we do... And Ricardo had his. During the days leading up to his trip, he thought about all the different types of women he liked, and he decided that the experience he wanted to start with in Amsterdam would be with a thin small-breasted woman, preferably Asian. But any nationality would do, as long as she was petite, with a small firm ass and tiny breasts. So when he went wandering through the red light district on his first night out in Amsterdam, that's the type he went looking for.

Now, I don't know why he thought he wanted that particular type, but he always claimed that Asian prostitutes were nicer. I think it was because his first few experiences in a brothel happened when he was quite young, still a teenager. And they happened in a brothel that was staffed by Asian women... but he always claimed they were better—that the Asian prostitutes took their time with you, caressed you, kissed you, made you feel happy, and eventually when you did have your orgasm, they didn't rush you out the door. He claimed they made you feel loved. Now, I think his first prostitutes probably did treat him better because he was so young...

ha, young and probably scared... and maybe because they were Asian, and they were so nice to him, and they were all petite with tiny breasts, that somehow that look, that type, got imprinted on his brain. Anyway, somehow Ricardo was trying to recreate that type of experience in Amsterdam—that feeling of being loved... and of course that's what it was really all about, you know, deep down underneath. The sex that Ricardo was looking for was something that would make him feel loved... because this growing malaise that he had been experiencing for so many months was the malaise that comes from not feeling loved, or to be more accurate, from not feeling lovable... but... I digress.

Anyway, so Ricardo set off that night in Amsterdam looking for a petite prostitute with tiny breasts and a small tight ass. Well... you've been to Amsterdam, so you know that those types are actually hard to find. Most of the women there are busty types, usually from silicone or breast implants. It's simple economics that drives that body type. Almost 100% of the clients of the Amsterdam prostitutes are foreign men, and most of them prefer women with large breasts, and so most of the prostitutes have their breasts enlarged because that makes them more money. You know how strange it is to walk through the red light district there and see window after window showcasing almost identical-looking women: tall, dyed-blonde hair, and large breasts... Yes, well that was Ricardo's experience, too. He must have walked around through all those narrow winding streets for over an hour, passing by window after window of tall busty blondes or busty brunettes... but finally he came to a window that had a short petite woman with small breasts. She wasn't Asian, and of course her hair was dyed a very white blonde. But it was cut short, and she was cute. And as I said, petite with small breasts. And she smiled at Ricardo, but of course all the prostitutes smile at all the men who walk by. Nonetheless, she was the closest person he had found to that image in his head. So he walked by her window again, took a second look, and then stepped up to the door, which she opened, and then he stepped inside, and she drew the curtain.

Now, when I say she was cute, well, she was very cute, and she and Ricardo chatted for a bit. She told him she was from Bulgaria, which should have been a tip-off to him—many exploited women from Eastern Europe come to Amsterdam to make as much money as possible for either their family back home, or in many cases, their pimps back home. The Netherland tax structure is such that the first 14,000 Euros that a sex worker makes is tax-free; and 14,000 Euros is a huge amount of money in Bulgaria. So, many of these girls come to Amsterdam and work for four or five months a year, just until they make that tax-free maximum, and then they return to their Eastern European country of origin for the rest of the year. So it should have been a tip-off to Ricardo. But, like I say, she was cute. She asked him what he was looking for and he told her he liked touching, holding, cuddling and some sex. She told him the price of a session was 50 Euros, but Ricardo knew it would be 100 Euros before he was through. You know how it is in Amsterdam, yes? How the girls all say 50 Euros, but when you're naked and on the bed, suddenly it's an extra 50 Euros to complete the act? Yes, I assumed you'd know these things too. And Ricardo knew how it worked, so he wasn't surprised after he had gotten undressed and lay on the bed and asked her to get completely naked too, that she told him that having her naked and having a complete sex act would be an extra 50 Euros. They always do it that way because, well... what man quibbles when they're naked? So Ricardo forked over the extra 50

Euros and she took off her tiny top bra and underwear. And in fact, she did have a perfect body—just the kind of body that fit the image in Ricardo's head: perky tiny breasts, smooth skin over a muscular body, tiny ass... He gently reached up and cupped one of her breasts—it was soft and pointy, just what he liked. But that's when it got a little strange. Ricardo paid her what he thought was a compliment—he told her that the reason he had chosen her was because she wasn't surgically enhanced, that she was "natural". And she answered by saying, "How do you know my breasts aren't enhanced?" And it wasn't said as a way of making conversation—it was said more as a slight rebuke. Now it's true, they could have been enhanced, but Ricardo thought it odd that a prostitute would be arguing with a client over what was intended as a compliment. But he let it slide. In the meantime, he noticed that she was putting on a latex glove on one of her hands. She squeezed something into the gloved hand and then started to massage his cock. Some type of mild lubricant, Ricardo figured, but the touching of course made him start to get erect. Then she rolled a condom over his cock, all without saying another word, but then she took off the glove and took a paper towel with a hole in the middle and placed it over his cock, so that his cock poked up through the hole. Ricardo propped himself up on his elbows and looked at this— he had never seen this with a prostitute before, or with any woman for that matter. It looked more like a dental procedure. Then she positioned herself at the foot of the bed, between Ricardo's legs, but far enough down where he could not reach her with his hands, and proceeded to blow him. Now, that was enjoyable of course, but not exactly what Ricardo had wanted. He had already told her that he liked cuddling and touching, and she was going straight for the fast orgasm. Then at one point he started to reach down to grab the base of his cock and she said, "Don't touch the condom. I don't know where your hands have been." Now it became clear to Ricardo that this particular prostitute was rather germ-phobic: the latex gloves, the lack of touching, the paper around his genitals so that she had a buffer between any part of him and her, and of course the condom—although Ricardo understood the condom rule.

Then she said to him, "Do you want to fuck?" And Ricardo figured that maybe fucking her might be more pleasant than simply having her blow him, so he said yes, and she hopped off the bed, grabbed a small tube of lubricant, squeezed some into her hand and rubbed it up inside her pussy, climbed on top of Ricardo and guided his cock up inside her.

Now, most prostitutes prefer to fuck a client sitting on top of them. That puts them in control. They control the rhythm, which means they control the orgasm. And while it does give the man a nice visual view, it also removes any full body contact. So while this woman fit the image in Ricardo's head, the experience did not. Even though he was fucking her, there was not much touching going on, and certainly no loving caresses, which is what he really wanted. And then, when he reached his hands up to touch her breasts, she pushed his hands away, claiming it tickled too much. Well, that pretty much killed the whole experience for Ricardo. Here was a rather abrasive, germ-phobic prostitute who didn't enjoy touching or being touched by men, who was probably forced to do this for a living either because of economics or exploitation or whatever... but clearly, she didn't enjoy it. She was just not cut out to be a prostitute. And Ricardo was not enjoying the experience. Now, most men would never have the nerve in the middle of fucking someone to say, "You know, this isn't working out." But Ricardo didn't have any qualms about saying that since he was paying for the time. Plus, he figured that the sooner he left, the happier she would be. So he told her, albeit politely, but she understood, and hopped right off him, and started washing her hands. Ricardo got dressed as quickly as he could and left. Ironically, just as he was leaving, he heard her digital alarm clock go off. He realized that she had set it at the beginning of the session, just after he had paid her the second 50 Euros—his 15 minutes was up. What perfect timing, he thought ruefully.

But he was glad to be back out on the street, in the cool night air. The coolness of the evening seemed to be saying to him, *It's okay, step back into the night. Just walk around, relax, and let that experience go.* And so he just walked around, mulling over the disappointment, trying to not regret his actions, but rather, figure out what he could have done to prevent it. But it got to him, you know... First, the disappointment at Jimmy's gay bathhouse and now this disappointment with a woman. So his thoughts were swirling in his head. And you know how the cobblestone streets all curve, twist and turn, in the red light district? How you can walk there for hours? Anyway, he's walking around rather aimlessly, just thinking to himself... and you know how there are certain streets there dedicated to certain types of experiences? Particularly down around Bloedstraat? Ha, yes, you are correct, my friend, that's where all the trans sex workers are, the she-males. How did I know you would know that, eh? Well, Ricardo hadn't planned it, but he found himself down in that area, and he passed by one window, and there was this woman waving at him—she looked Spanish—and he slowed his walk a bit, and she lifted her tiny skirt and showed a bulge in her panties. That's when Ricardo noticed that her doorway had a blue light rather than the red light, indicating that she was a transvestite prostitute.

Well, Ricardo certainly didn't feel like parting with another 100 Euros, but on the other hand, the whole reason he had decided to stay an extra day or two in Amsterdam was to immerse himself in sex. So he walked up to the window.

Now, he wasn't exactly sure why he was doing this—because the sexual experience he had told himself he was looking for was with a woman—and yet here he was, walking up to talk to a she-male... which further supports my theory that people just don't know what they want... and it's not that this would have been a new experience for him... after all, you've read his books, so you know he was, shall we say... versatile? In fact, more than a decade earlier, before Phillipe had had her surgery, she and Ricardo had been lovers back in Hamburg. And of course, Ricardo had been with many men... It was just, as I said, he had convinced himself that what he needed on this trip was sex with women... and yet here he was, walking up to talk to a transvestite prostitute.

And the fact is, Ricardo did love women. Women have a softness, even the muscular ones, a soft quality, a smoothness of skin and soul, that always melted him. In fact, I think he worshipped women. He loved touching them, and being touched by them. There's something about it, don't you think? Touching a man is just something altogether different—it's a different energy, a different sexuality, a different feeling. But transvestites somehow bridge those two—they have some of the energy, some of the soft touch, of a woman... but, with a cock.

Anyway, as Ricardo was walking up to the doorway of this she-male, he thought to himself, *Well, she's not a woman, but she's my next best option,* and the she-male opened her door and Ricardo stepped inside. She was not petite—most she-males aren't—she had muscular shoulders but her breasts were not overly enhanced, and Ricardo liked the way she looked. She said her name was Marilyn and she was from Seville, Spain. And maybe that's what did the trick. Because, as I said, Ricardo was originally trying to recreate that imprinted image of the Asian prostitutes he had had as a teenager, but he had also had his share of Spanish prostitutes when he was in his twenties. So there was maybe enough imagery there to make Marilyn acceptable to Ricardo that night. Anyway, they chatted, and Ricardo asked her if she was "fully-functional," meaning of course, could she get an erection, and she assured him she could, so he nodded his head in agreement to the deal, and she pulled the curtain across the window in the door.

He asked her how much, and unlike most of the prostitutes in Amsterdam, she said 100 Euros for 40 minutes. This, as you know, is unusual. Disclosing the full amount up front was unusual, and contracting for a full 40 minutes for that amount was also unusual—that's more than twice the amount of time that 100 Euros would buy with a female prostitute there. But it's because the trans prostitutes don't get as much business as the women, so they have to try and create repeat customers. Anyway, Ricardo paid her, and she led him into the bedroom. She pointed to a chair and told him he could put his clothes there, and he began to undress. And she did the same. When she took off her bra, Ricardo liked what he saw. Some transvestites get horrible breast surgery, trying to make their breasts too big and end up with either rock hard breasts or nasty scars. But Marilyn had only added small breasts, and there were few scars and the breasts were soft and natural looking. And when she slipped off her panties, Ricardo was even more pleased—she had a nice looking cock.

They both stood there naked looking at each other. Then Marilyn stepped forward and they hugged. Ricardo could feel her breasts against his upper stomach and her cock pushing against his cock. She actually kissed his neck—again, most unusual to get any kissing from a prostitute in Amsterdam.

She pulled away and pointed to the bed, and he lay down. She lay down beside him and they hugged some more. Ricardo ran his hands over her back and down around her muscular ass. He bent down and kissed her breasts, licking the large nipples. He was amazed at how natural her breasts felt. She reached down and started playing with his cock and he reached down and started playing with her cock. Both she and Ricardo started to get hard.

"Would you like me to suck your cock?" she asked him.

"Can I suck yours?" Ricardo responded.

"Of course," she said, and sat up on the bed on her knees bringing her cock up to his face.

"With a condom," Ricardo said.

"Of course," she said, and reached over to box of condoms on the nightstand by the bed and rolled one on herself.

And so Ricardo started to suck her, while reaching up and feeling her breasts, and she responded. Her cock got harder and harder. That's another interesting difference between the female prostitutes and the trans prostitutes, don't you think? That the female prostitutes will fake being excited by a client by moaning and groaning, but the trans prostitutes can't fake an erection. The fact was, Marilyn was getting hard, and this only excited Ricardo more.

At this point, Marilyn was still standing on her

knees on the bed beside Ricardo, who was lying prone on his side, and he was blowing her, that is, he was doing the action. But then she pushed him over on his back and sort of laid over him and she started fucking his mouth rather forcefully. Her cock was now fully erect and at various times Ricardo had to force himself not to gag. She wasn't being rough, but at the same time, she was basically raping his mouth. And in spite of the gagging, he was loving it. This went on for several minutes, her fucking his mouth and him running his hands over her breasts and around her ass. Finally, after almost gagging a lot, Ricardo pushed her pelvis back and her cock out of his mouth, and gasped for breath.

She leaned over and brought her breasts to his face and he sucked on each nipple for a bit.

Then she whispered, "Do you want me to fuck you?"

"Yes," he softly answered.

She got up and took a large pump bottle of lubricant and spread lube over her condom. Then she told Ricardo to stand by the bed, with his back to her and bend over the bed. Ricardo did as he was told, his feet on the floor, bent over the bed, and resting his forearms on the bed for support. Marilyn approached him from behind, forced some lube up his ass with her finger, and then eased her cock into his ass and began to slowly fuck him.

Now, I have no idea, of course, what women experience when someone fucks their vagina. But I think it must be a very different experience than what a man feels being fucked in the ass. There is just—I don't know how to describe it—but there is just a certain ghastly thrill to having another man force his lubed cock up your ass. You know what I'm talking about? Yes, I can see you do. Some people theorize that it's because the act is so taboo. The religious zealots of course claim that God designed vaginas for fucking and rectums for shitting, and many scientists claim that these two different anatomical features evolved for their very different functions. But I don't know. Maybe God designed the ass to serve a double purpose. I mean, think about the tongue—it serves many different purposes, from talking to tasting to licking the lips to sticking down someone's throat... Maybe the ass evolved to be fucked as well as to shit. After all, why are there so many pleasure nerves around the asshole? All the scientists and religious nuts always ignore that question. What is the function of all those pleasure nerves if not for pleasure? Why have people been fucking each other in the ass since the beginning of time? Obviously, people enjoy giving oral sex and receiving anal sex because the body experiences pleasure in those activities. Why would the human body evolve— or be created—to experience pleasure by sucking another man's cock or by being fucked by another man? Who's to say that the ass wasn't designed or didn't evolve to serve double-duty, so to speak? I don't know—I am neither religious nor scientific. I only know that people do these things; people have always done these things; and people will always do these things. You know what I mean, don't you? Yes...

At any rate, Ricardo certainly enjoyed it. Marilyn was pounding away and he could feel her cock going way up, in and out, of his ass. She was fucking him hard. He was stroking himself with his right hand and had his left arm extended straight out, pushing against the bed to brace himself against her fucking. You know how good sex takes control of your body and your mind? How you go into some other zone where you have no control and often can't remember anything? Well, Ricardo was in that zone. He had totally lost control of himself as Marilyn was fucking him, and suddenly he realized he was about to cum. He let out a loud moan, squirted three large orgasmic spurts across the side of the bed, and then simply collapsed onto the bed, into his own cum, as Marilyn pulled out of him. He lay there just moaning softly as she pulled the condom off her still erect cock and threw it into a small trash can by the bed. Then she grabbed one of those wet paper napkins—I don't know what you call them... I think baby wipes—from a box and wiped off her cock, and threw that wet napkin in the trash as well. Then she grabbed another wet napkin and walked up to Ricardo, who was still sprawled over the bed, and used it to wipe his ass, to clean any lubricant off his ass. The cold wetness of the napkin helped bring Ricardo's mind back to where he was. It was then that he noticed that the bed was covered with a fitted plastic sheet. That's good, he thought, because he hadn't meant to cum over Marilyn's bed. At least he didn't stain any sheets. He slowly peeled himself up off the bed. Marilyn handed him another wet napkin and he wiped the cum off his stomach and off his cock. She handed him another one, and he wiped his cum off the plastic sheet. As he threw the napkins into the trash, he could not help but notice how many condoms and used napkins were in the trash can. That also helped to bring him back to reality.

And that reality was that it was time for him to go. Marilyn was already putting her bra and panties and tiny skirt back on. So Ricardo grabbed his underwear off the chair and started getting dressed as well.

"Marilyn," he said, "that was just fantastic. You're amazing."

"Amo el sexo," she said. "I do love the sex."

"Yes," Ricardo said softly. "Yes, so do I."

"Then you come back to see me again, yes?"

"Yes, I will."

He finished getting dressed. When he was ready to leave, Marilyn gave him a light kiss on the lips, pulled back the curtain, and opened the door for him. Ricardo stepped back out into the cool night air and walked back to his hotel room. And as he walked back he thought about the irony of that night: his original goals were to have sex with a skinny woman, and to feel loved... and he had achieved both goals, but with two different people. Who says the gods don't have a sense of humor, eh?

Chapter 6: The Water of ife

Such a fine wine. I think I may order another bottle, if you don't mind. You don't have an early flight out tomorrow do you? No? Three more days here? Really? Excellent. You'll join me in another glass of wine then, yes? Good. *Garçon, une autre bouteille, s'il vous plaît.*

So, my young friend, are you getting a sense of the kind of man that Ricardo is... or rather, was... last June? Do you see why I said earlier that some people think of him as debauched? I know you've read his books, so you knew he was sexual, but his books don't tell the whole story. The fact is, Ricardo thought about sex all the time. For him, sex was the water of life, and he could think of nothing else except bringing the vessel to his lips and drinking deep until he could quench his thirst. The problem of course, is that the thirst for sex can never be quenched. One temporarily gets one's fill, but the next day, the craving returns. Sex is a fountain, alright—it's the fountain that keeps on giving... or taking... depending on your point of view.

You know, it's kind of ironic, in a way... Ricardo had originally intended to spend a few days in Amsterdam indulging all these *different* sexual fantasies, *different* women, *different* places... When he was in New York, thinking ahead to Amsterdam, he created a little map in his mind... except that instead of a tourist map, it was a sexual map... he thought about how he would start by trying to find a petite Asian woman, and then maybe the next night visit the gay bathhouses, and then a different hooker the following night, and then maybe the night after that he might try one of the sex clubs. He had it all planned out... but you know what they say about the best-laid plans... or maybe about the best plans for getting laid... Ha!... but anyway, Ricardo never did dive into the sexual buffet table of Amsterdam, sampling all the exotic dishes... No, he simply went back to Marilyn for the next two nights... This, of course, just underscores my point that no one really knows what they want...

"Well hello, sailor," Marilyn said when she opened her door to him the next night. "Come on in."

Ricardo stepped inside and Marilyn pulled the curtain shut over the window. "Couldn't stay away?" she said with a smile and reached down between Ricardo's legs and rubbed the outside of his pants over his cock.

"No I couldn't," Ricardo said, and gave her a hug. Then he reached into his pocket, and took out 200 Euros that he had put there before he left his hotel, handed it to her and said, "Let's play for awhile tonight, try some different things."

She looked at the money, took it, and said, "I'm all yours, baby."

You know, I remember once Ricardo quipped to me that sex was the strongest aphrodisiac in the world. But in a way I think he was right. There's nothing quite as addictive as really good sex, is there? George Gurdjieff, the Armenian mystic, claimed that for every man, there was one woman out of 628 who would be the perfect sexual partner for him, someone whose mere physical nature would drive him to ecstasy. One out of 628... Ha, I don't know where he got that figure... maybe it was just his way of explaining why most men never find that perfect sexual partner, I don't know. And I'm not saying that Marilyn was that for Ricardo—no, she was not that for him—but she did a good job of getting him excited. On that return visit, for his 200 Euros, she tied him up so he couldn't move, then lay on top of him in a 69 position, her full weight on him, and fucked his mouth while blowing him. She was not a petite trans and he told me later that he could barely breathe, but he loved it. Then she switched positions, tied his legs apart, and fucked him until he came... You know, letting someone tie you up and fuck you requires a great deal of trust, don't you think? Yes, I can see you know what I'm talking about, and I think that was part of the instant chemistry between them—that kind of trust. The following night, he went back again, and Marilyn fucked him again... which is really weird, because Ricardo wasn't normally a bottom. He much preferred being a top. But that, as the pop song says, that's the power of love... ha! More like the magnetic power of sex... but, to be accurate, it really wasn't the sex that kept Ricardo coming back, because the experiences with Marilyn—assuming that was her real name, which it probably wasn't —but those experience seemed to ease Ricardo's depression substantially. He went back to his hotel and slept well each night, and woke up each morning feeling refreshed.

On the morning after his third visit to Marilyn, he went out and found a quiet café and ordered breakfast. And after breakfast, he lingered there over coffee and thought over each of the three previous nights in detail. He was aware that he felt good—that his body felt relaxed, vibrant. He recognized this feeling—it was how he felt after a night of sex with someone he loved. Even though what had actually happened was that he was banged up the ass by a transvestite hooker three nights in row, that particular morning his body and emotions tingled with the exact same exuberant relaxed sensorial joy as if he had made love all night to a woman he was totally in love with. Life felt good to him. And it struck him as very odd that he should feel this way—that he should feel so good. And so, because he was a writer, and therefore a thinker, he sat there in that café and thought about that, analyzed it, deconstructed it, tried to figure it out.

He began thinking about why there was so little love in his life. He wondered what it was about the sex with Marilyn that seemed to have restored him a bit. Because, you see, Ricardo had had many evenings in his life that consisted of hot sex with complete strangers... in the bathhouses or the brothels... and he usually left those places feeling satiated... but also still feeling sad, empty, and alone...but the morning after being with Marilyn was different—and he realized that he almost felt... for that short time with her... he almost felt a hint of caring *from her*, a semblance of love, or respect, or decency toward him and his desires... He wasn't sure what it was, but he was clear that it wasn't the sex that made him feel better—it was Marilyn's *attitude* towards him. She was trans and was perfectly okay with another man wanting to suck her cock or be fucked by her. And her acceptance of that—specifically, her acceptance of Ricardo wanting that—felt like love to Ricardo.

And what is love, really? It's the respect that someone shows you, the decency with which they treat you when you expose your most private thoughts and desires to them. The desires and secret fantasies that we have as humans, well... they are so personal and so wanton, so *undignified,* that we are ashamed of them, and it takes only the slightest molecule of scorn or reproach from another person to make us close up like an armadillo and cover ourselves with our hard shell again... and I'm not just talking about sexual desire—any private thought or secret part of our soul is just as easily wounded. Only love can accept these hideous thoughts and desires. Only love allows us to open like flowers and expose ourselves and grow. You know... the Catholic Church knew this and exploited this fact quite well for centuries. You step into a dark room and share your most inner thoughts and deeds, the most horrible and private things imaginable, and then a person imbued with some authority accepts that and absolves you. No wonder the people kept coming back to church. The confession, when it was done right, gave them what no lover ever could: total acceptance and absolution. But I digress. I tend to do that with a good wine and good company. People say I'm quite a talker... I hope you don't mind. Oh, well, that's kind of you to say. Thank you.

Where was I? Oh yes, I was going to say that I think where Ricardo had gotten confused was that he was so focused on sex... well, no, that's not right... what I mean is that he was very focused on sex because he had always known that for him it was the water of life... for him it explained everything... and because he was so focused on that energy, he got confused into thinking that love had to be equally focused on sex the same way he was. By that I mean, that Ricardo assumed that any long-term partner, any lover, would have to be equally focused on sex, and would have to be accepting of his sexual interests. I mean, it sounds logical, doesn't it? Don't we all want partners who accept us as we are? But that's the ironic thing about love. He could have fallen in love with someone who loved him deeply, who accepted him deeply, but who wasn't as focused on sex as he was, or didn't necessarily accept his sexual peccadilloes. Odd, isn't it, that love, the experience that we yearn for because it's so accepting, can still be pure love and not be accepting. That's the problem with us humans, you know—we want love on our terms, but love doesn't give a fuck about our terms. I don't know how people think of love anymore—how they conceptualize it—we've become such a fragmented world... but I think love is an energy that floats around us like a cloud, it drifts through the streets like smoke, and occasionally we happen to stroll down a certain street and start inhaling, and the next thing we know, we're chatting up some person who happened to be walking down that same street, and we find them pleasant to chat with, and so we ask if they'd like to sit and chat some more over a drink or coffee, and one thing leads to another... but that's just my theory. I don't know what Ricardo thought love was, except that he thought a lot about it, and that he thought it was both wonderful and horrible, and that he feared that it had left him forever.

I remember, years ago, reading an interview with Mother Teresa where she talked about a time when she felt that God had withdrawn all love from her—and for her, God's love was a type of sensorial contact—and she described how alone and abandoned she felt. She simply could not contact God. Now, I'm not drawing comparisons between Ricardo and Mother Teresa here... Ricardo was no saint... but I only mention it so as to illustrate Ricardo's experience—that he felt that love had withdrawn from his life, that he had no way to contact love. Of course, he was rather handicapped in that his only methods of communication were sexual. Nonetheless, he felt that love had evaporated from his life, and that at his age, he would never find someone to love again.

And there's a certain actuarial truth to that, you know. Ricardo was no spring chicken. Ha! twenty-year-olds totally ignored him; thirty-year-olds called him "sir"; and even forty-year-olds held the door for him. To be honest, that's why he frequented prostitutes—it was only there that he could hope to touch younger flesh again.

Anyway, so there Ricardo was, sitting over coffee, mulling over these things, and it began to dawn on him that the lack of love in his life was due, in part, to his only seeking love in sex. That is, he began to realize these things I'm telling you right now, that love comes to us in many forms... but it's not a constant... it can disappear for awhile... like it did for Mother Teresa, as it does when people age, and as it had done for Ricardo... but it disappears only because it's drifting around somewhere else, like smoke... It drifts through the streets we walk in and the cafés we sit in... and floats around us, and it doesn't give a damn if we don't see it or receive it... love doesn't exist for us, you know; it has its own life... we're just lucky—or unlucky—innocent bystanders.

Now, Ricardo was not going to give up sex. Not by any means, but there was something in that experience with Marilyn that triggered the thought—or rather, connected the dots—that maybe the reason that he felt such a lack of love in his life was because he was only open to receiving it through sex. Now, I know that sounds obvious... all insights are obvious once you see them. But like all insights, the sudden flash of it illuminates the world a little bit. At any rate, Ricardo latched onto this thought. Like I said, he wasn't going to give up on sex, but he wondered if he been blind to the full spectrum of love.

And because this thought was in his mind, as he walked from the café back to the hotel, he started looking at people in the street. You know Amsterdam, how crowded the streets are. Full of tourists, all walking with backpacks or fanny packs, or luggage on wheels. It can be a real hassle to try and walk somewhere fast in Amsterdam, right? Normally you have to zigzag your way through the crowds, so you're focused on the openings in the crowd, the spaces between people, as you walk, not actually looking at the people themselves. But on this particular morning, because of how he was feeling, because this thought about love was in his mind, Ricardo walked slowly, and just looked at the people. And what he saw amazed him.

He saw this tiny Japanese girl struggling up the stairs on one of those stairways below the street that leads to a hotel—she was struggling with this oversized heavy suitcase... and a man on the street, a complete stranger to her, stopped, went down the stairs and simply helped her carry her suitcase up, and then at the top of the stairs, she thanked him profusely, and he just smiled and went on his way.

He saw a mother and father slowly pushing a grown woman, probably their daughter, in a wheelchair. The woman was obviously paralyzed, but the parents were totally focused on her, talking to her and pointing out the different buildings and sights, and the crowds of people all around them, almost instinctively, would create a space to let them pass through.

He saw a woman drop a scarf and another woman ran to it, picked it up, and ran after the woman, tapped her on the shoulder, and handed her the scarf, telling her she had dropped it.

He saw two women walking along, using sign language to talk to each other, both smiling and enjoying the day. A stranger walking the opposite way saw them, smiled, and signed "hello" to them as he walked by and they smiled and signed "hello" back.

He saw an old man walking slowly across the street with a cane, walking so slowly that the crosswalk light started to turn red, but all the cars and motorcycles and bicyclists simply waited patiently, without honking, for him to complete his journey across the street.

He saw tourists in the canal boats, taking the one-hour cruise through the canals, snapping pictures and pointing to all the sights they had never seen before, and all feeling a sense of community with their fellow strangers on that boat.

And all of those sights happened within the first 5 minutes of Ricardo's walk back to the hotel! And Ricardo was stunned. I mean, it's not that there weren't negative things in the street, too. There are always negative things—dog shit in the street, drunks sleeping in the corners, drug dealers lurking in the alleys, cars honking, people looking unhappy, and tons of fat tourists loaded down with bags of useless things they had purchased... but what stunned Ricardo was all the kindness that he had never seen before, co-existing along with the negativity. And so he delayed his return to his hotel and just wandered about the streets, deliberately trying to only focus on acts of kindness. It takes a bit of effort, you know, because there really is so much negativity in the world. But he found that if he looked for these little moments of kindness—and it took a deliberate effort to focus on them—but that if he looked for these little moments of kindness, he could spot them. They appear like flashes of light in the river of time. If you blink, the moment passes and you can miss them completely. Ha, you know, he told me later he felt like he was playing Pokémon Go—you know that game the young people play on their cell phones? Yes, well he thought he was searching for Kindnessmon... and what he noticed was that every time he spotted one, it made him feel good. It gave him a microscopic jolt of that same feeling of pleasure he had felt from Marilyn. Odd, isn't it? There was nothing sexual about it. But then, as I said, it wasn't the sex with Marilyn that made him feel good... it was the *respect* that Marilyn gave him.

So anyway, Ricardo was just meandering around the streets, doing this experiment of trying to see kindness, when at one point, something happened. He had come to a corner and was just standing there, deliberating which street to turn down, or whether to head back to his hotel, when a couple approached him. It was a man and a woman, both Asian, both pulling those suitcases on wheels. And the woman said to him in broken English, "Excuse me, we are lost. Do you know where the Tulip Hotel is?"

Ricardo didn't know this particular hotel, so he asked, "Do you know the address?" And the woman pulled out a small notebook and showed him the page where she had written down the address.

Now Ricardo was generally familiar with Amsterdam, but he had also picked up a tourist map from the hotel desk that morning and had stuck it in his back pocket. So he pulled out the map and opened it, found the street that the lady had written down, and then he recognized the street. It was a popular street where there were many decent tourist hotels, and he figured that the hotel would be there.

He pointed to the map, and said, "We are here, at this corner. Your hotel is on this street." Then he pointed to the next corner, one block away. "You need to go to that corner, turn left, walk five blocks and then turn right."

The woman and the man both looked at the map, and Ricardo repeated the directions slowly.

"The hotel will be on that street. Just ask someone there."

And then Ricardo gave them the map, saying, "Here, take this."

And the couple's eyes widened a bit, but they took the map, and thanked him several times and walked away, pulling their luggage.

Now this is an event that happens a hundred times a day in Amsterdam—tourists asking directions— and the map was easy to give away. Ricardo's hotel had a whole stack of them. So it cost him nothing, but it made the couple feel good. And it made him feel good, too... he told me later that it made him feel like a better person. And again, he had that tiny microscopic jolt of energy.

So all these things were swirling around in his brain as he walked back to his hotel.

Love is a fragile thing, you know, because thinking too much about it kills it. We are even taking risks talking about it tonight, because talking creates thinking, so perhaps I should not mention it any more tonight.

So I will tell you only this: That Ricardo was thinking very seriously about these things, thinking very seriously about the nature of love... And to illustrate my point about why thinking kills love... let me point out that he was thinking about the nature of love because he had been fucked in the ass, okay? I mean, consider the paradox here... he was thinking about the pure absolution of love because some tranny hooker had shoved her lubricated cock up Ricardo's rectum... you see the paradox? Yes? Ah, yes, I see you do.

So anyway, that what was in his brain in Amsterdam that day, as he walked back to his hotel.

Ah, and here comes the waiter with our bottle of wine. I was wondering what was taking him so long. Maybe he had to go way down to the cellar.

Chapter 7: Kindness

Here, let me refill your glass. Now, where was I? Oh yes, so... Ricardo was turning these things over in his mind that morning, all these thoughts about kindness and love, and about the lack of love being related to the lack of kindness, and then he asked himself the one question that most people never ask after they have an insight... Most of the time, you know, we have an insight, and that brief flash of awareness illuminates our world for a second, but then the light dims, and the insight, as the old psalm goes, dies as a dream dies at opening day... unless one asks the simple question: How can I put this into action? But Ricardo *did* ask himself that question, and the answer that came to him... well, when I say it, it will seem as obvious and as simplistic as when I described his insight... but it had never been obvious to Ricardo before... the answer that came to him was that he had to talk to people. But let me explain: Ricardo knew how to talk to people. After all, he was a writer, so his skill was with words. And he was educated, so he could talk about a variety of things. But his talking to people had always been goal-oriented... hmm, how to explain? There had always been some objective, some agenda that he had in talking to people. He wanted to seduce some woman or some man; or he wanted help; or he needed information about something. He was an American, so there was always a purpose behind everything he did—it was part of his cultural heritage. But now he wondered what would happen if he just reached out and talked to someone without wanting anything from them, but wanting only to demonstrate—to create—a little bit of love and respect for them. It's a subtle thing, you know. It's the difference between saying to someone "That's a nice jacket" and "That's a nice jacket; where did you get it?" The first sentence is just a compliment. The second is envy and has the object of finding out where the shop is that sells that type of jacket so that you can get one yourself. They're both legitimate—nothing wrong with either one—but they're different.

So he's thinking about this as he is walking back to his hotel, and he's crossing one of the canals, and standing at the railing by the canal is a middle-aged couple, obviously tourists. The man had just taken a photo of the canal, and the boats... and they were just standing there admiring the scene. And Ricardo stopped a few feet from where they were standing, and looked. And he saw what they were seeing, which was that it was a beautiful view, a lovely view. And then he turned to them and said, "It's beautiful, isn't it?" And they both turned to him and smiled and then the woman said, in a British accent, "Yes, it is." And the couple looked at him, and he looked at the couple, and they both smiled and nodded their heads, and then went their separate ways... It's a simple thing, you know, a kind word, a kind gesture... Sometimes it's only just that—just that simple moment... less than a second, really... but it takes a tremendous amount of energy to be alert to these moments and to seize them and turn them into a microsecond of human contact, doesn't it? Yes, it does.

Now, I don't mean to paint a simple picture here... I have spoken about this kindness thing at length only to try and identify it for you, but the fact is, we humans are not that simple. Every civilization, every culture, and every person knows that we are each both devil and saint... both demon and angel... at the exact same time.

So I don't mean to in any way suggest that Ricardo had some sort of epiphany with Marilyn that forever changed his life... I mean, in a way, it did... but it simply is not that simple... Life is never that simple... We humans are more like oceans than we are like islands, you know. Islands are self-contained, but oceans have all these currents, all these levels, all happening at the same time... That's the thing about the human mind, the human psyche, is that there are all these simultaneous events, occurring not only in our minds, but in our actual lives, all happening at once. And so it was with Ricardo. There he was in Amsterdam that morning, wandering the streets, feeling the glow of post-coital love from a transvestite prostitute—whose real name he didn't even know—but feeling it nonetheless, walking around, trying to discover the meaning of kindness and how it relates to love, trying to figure out how to actually apply that in his life, that is, how to be more kind. And while all that is going on, he's wondering where he can get more sex, when he's going to fly to Spain, whether he's should go to Madrid first because the bathhouses and the prostitutes are better or whether he should go to Barcelona first because that was the whole reason he came to Europe... It's the strangest thing—the human mind—I really do think it's like an ocean: very cold and dark at the bottom, where these strange creatures swim, and then above, all these layers of temperatures and currents, even riptides, all moving in different directions, and then at the very top, either a beautiful view or a horrible storm... I mean, I'm no psychologist, but to me it's a wonder we get anything done with all the different currents going on inside us.

But I wanted to describe for you this particular current that was flowing in Ricardo's ocean that day— this current of actually trying to be kind... actually trying to make contact with people... because later that current made such a difference in what happened to him. So just bear in mind, when I relate what happened over the next few days, that despite all his observable actions, underneath, somewhere deep down in the depths, these thoughts about kindness were gathering strength. They were gathering their own strength apart from him, and they were beginning to move in a certain path, despite his actions far above on the surface of the waves of his life.

So... okay... so the time came for him to leave Amsterdam... and he decided— and I think he would agree it was simply a selfish decision—he decided to fly to Madrid first, spend a few days there, and then fly to Barcelona... Now I need to explain a bit, perhaps... You know that Madrid is Castilian and Barcelona is Catalonian, right? Two different kingdoms—two different cultures and heritages and genetics—that were united into Spain in 1492 when Queen Isabella of Castile married King Ferdinand of Catalonia... right? And while both regions have been the country of Spain since that time, they really are quite distinct regions... Okay, I see you are familiar with this. Now, Ricardo loved both areas: He loved Barcelona because he was born there, and he loved Madrid because he became a man there. Say what? Well, by that I mean that... well, let's just say that while he was born in Barcelona, it was in Madrid that he discovered sex... but that's another story... Personally speaking, I prefer Barcelona. It's more progressive. But Ricardo preferred Madrid. Now, I disagree with him on this. But in his opinion, the women in Madrid were more beautiful. But I do have to agree with him that the gay bathhouses in Madrid are better. Now I don't know if that entered into Ricardo's decision to go there first, but the fact is that he decided to go there first. So later that evening, he went online and booked a flight for the next morning and made a reservation in a small hotel.

Now, Madrid... Madrid... have you been there? Oh, really? How many times? Excellent, so you don't need me to tell you what a wonderfully complex—and sexual— city Madrid is. And in what neighborhood do you think Ricardo selected for his hotel? Yes, that's correct... in the Chueca neighborhood... and of course, he selected that neighborhood for the obvious reasons: they have the best gay bars, the best sex shops, and the best bathhouses and they are near the small brothels that line the Calle de la Montera.

But I'm getting ahead of myself... So the next morning Ricardo took the quick train ride from Amsterdam City Central to Schiphol Airport, and it was at the airport that he met the woman María Montagé... yes, *that* María Montagé... I see you have read the papers... well, actually it was inside the airplane, after he boarded, that he met her. He hadn't noticed her at the gate, but the fact was, she was there, also waiting for the same flight to Madrid. She had her one-year-old daughter Sophi with her. But it was only when Ricardo boarded the plane and took his assigned seat that he discovered that he was sitting next to María. There were two seats on that side of the plane—Ricardo had the aisle seat, and María was sitting in the window seat with Sophi on her lap.

Now, many people, especially Americans, abhor being seated next to a mother with a small baby. They are paranoid that the baby will cry and scream for the whole flight, and of course crying babies, like lots of real life things, bother many people, especially Americans. Why, I've even seen some Americans demand that they be given a different seat upon discovering that they have been seated next to a mother and a baby, just out of some paranoia that the baby might cry, or poop, or do those things that all babies do—which are all the same things those Americans did when they were babies. But on that particular morning, probably because of this undercurrent of kindness that had been circulating deep inside Ricardo, he didn't mind being seated next to María and Sophi. María was playing with Sophi when Ricardo reached the seat, and Sophi was laughing, and it gave Ricardo a warm feeling seeing that, and after he placed his backpack in the overhead bin, María looked up and smiled at him; and it was one of those smiles that was friendly yet still communicated just a hint of an apology, a hint of hope that he didn't mind sitting next to a mother and a baby; but as I said, Ricardo didn't mind, so he smiled back, and sat down beside her.

And again, that undercurrent of—I don't know what to call it, so I simply call it kindness—that undercurrent of kindness was still circulating in Ricardo, so he started talking to María. And I think it was in part because the baby was so beautiful. Big brown eyes and black curly hair around that chubby baby face, and smiling and laughing, and of course looking—you know how babies look, really look, at everything, actually taking in everything, all that they see... and Sophi was looking at Ricardo, wide-eyed and smiling that bubbly smile, and Ricardo just said out loud to both María and Sophi, "What a beautiful baby!" And that made María smile, because it meant that Ricardo accepted her, her with her one-year-old baby. And she and Ricardo fell into an easy conversation.

Ricardo told me later that it took him awhile to realize how pretty María was. You know how it is when you're sitting next to someone in an airplane—you're both facing the same direction, so you really can't look someone straight in the face—you're mostly talking sideways at each other, half-looking at each other, trying to manage that small space that airplanes cram you into these days. But they talked easily, and as they talked and warmed to each other, they both, unconsciously probably, turned to face each other more, to be able to see each other more.

María was of mixed heritage—just like Ricardo. And maybe that was the fact that intrigued Ricardo the most. María's mother was Colombian, but her father was Mexican-American, and she had been born in Los Angeles, California. Ricardo related to this, obviously, because his mother was Spanish and his father American, but they didn't discover this commonality until later in the flight, but when they did, it led them to compare notes about what it was like to have a foot in two different worlds. Most airplane conversations between strangers are just surface chit-chat, but Ricardo and María connected, probably because of this common mixed heritage, and they shared some of their personal experiences with racism and bigotry. All the while, of course, Sophi was laughing or playing, and María would alternate her attention and her words between Ricardo and Sophi.

Ricardo later described María to me. She wasn't particularly svelte, but she was not chubby either—she had a certain curvy body, not particularly tall. Her face was roundish, like Sophi's, and like Sophi she had big brown eyes, and full lips. Her face didn't have the classic Latina thin nose high-cheekbone look. It was softer, and in fact, if it wasn't for the café con leche color of her skin and her long black hair, you wouldn't have suspected she was Latina.

She told him she was on her way to Madrid, to try and reconcile with Sophi's father, a young Spaniard named Artemio. Evidently this Artemio lived in Madrid with his mother. María had met him two years earlier in the states. They both were students at some university in Southern California—I forget which one—and they had gotten involved, and María had gotten pregnant, but then the young man had returned to Spain. She and the guy had kept in touch via email, and although the man had seen Sophi via Skype, he had never seen his daughter in person. María told Ricardo enough that Ricardo understood that she was hoping to reunite with the young man, hoping his family would accept her, hoping that maybe they could marry, or at least live together and raise Sophi together.

The story seemed sad to Ricardo, and he felt some trepidation that María's hopes were going to be dashed, but he didn't want to say anything negative because she seemed so hopeful, so happy. But, of course, it seemed to Ricardo that if the young man hadn't made any effort to either return to the states or bring María over to Madrid earlier, that he was not going to be mature enough to marry her or help her raise Sophi. It's a story as old as time, you know, like all those old folk songs that date back to the Middle Ages: "wooed in haste, wed at leisure"... all those women down through the centuries, seduced with promises, with desire, and either because of love or lack of contraception or bad luck, they got pregnant, and then they got abandoned.

And so Ricardo asked her in a roundabout way about her family, hoping to learn enough about María's relationship with her own mother and father to reassure himself that she had some type of support system back in the states should her plans for the Madrid boy fall through, but all he learned was that her mother had passed away and her father had remarried and lived somewhere in Northern California. But he tried to tell himself that she would be okay, regardless of what happened. They continued to talk about their lives, and their travel plans. And again, I think that undercurrent of kindness was operating here, because on any other flight, at any other time, chatting with a pretty woman, Ricardo would have been flirting more, trying to figure out how he could seduce this person, trying to angle for some future contact in case her plans fell through, trying, in other words, to position himself, to gain some advantage. But he wasn't doing that on this day—he was just talking, and sharing, and listening, and respecting her.

And that's how the flight went. Ricardo and María chatted; Sophi played and laughed, and the two hour flight time passed quickly... too quickly and too soon they landed in Madrid, and it was time to disembark the plane. And so they did. And there at the airport, they said their goodbyes, and each wished the other well, and Sophi was smiling, and Ricardo left to catch a taxi, and María and Sophi went to catch a metro train to wherever she was going to meet that young man.

And in the cab ride to his hotel, Ricardo thought about María, and he said a silent prayer that things would work out for her, and he assumed that he would never see her again. And then he turned his attention to more earthly concerns.

He got to his hotel, checked in, unpacked his backpack, placed his passport, laptop, cell phone and wallet in his room safe, keeping out just enough Euros to cover his intended evening activities. And then later, after a late afternoon siesta, he went out into the cool evening to look for sex.

Ironically, even though he had originally intended to have all those different sexual experiences in Amsterdam, he ended up having them in Madrid. That first night, for example, after he left the hotel, and after he had grabbed a bite to eat at a local kebab shop, he stopped into a small bear bar in Chueca to have a beer—

you know those kind of bars—they cater to mostly older men, big burly men, or simply men past forty. You'd think it was a biker bar if it wasn't for the dark rooms in the basement with the gay porn playing. Anyway, Ricardo grabbed a beer there, just to loosen up after his kebab dinner, and he wandered through the dark basement rooms checking out the porn, and then headed over to the Primitivo Sauna. You know it? Ah yes, it's the best, isn't it? Well, Ricardo thought so too.

So he went there, and I guess this was the start of his surreal sexual experiences in Madrid... Well, let me explain. He went there—it was just down that side street about a eight-block walk from his hotel... and he knew the place, of course... and he paid his money, got his towel and locker key and went inside... and of course it was packed with men... You know, just on that thought, I wish that all women could see what happens in a gay bathhouse... because I think they would understand men so much more if they did. If they saw what happens in a bathhouse, they would appreciate the whole issue that men have with erections. Women always assume that their own bodies are enough to give men an erection. They assume that if they take their clothes off and expose their naked beauty to a man, he will of course respond with an erection. It's a beautiful thought, but of course you know, it's not true. Erections require constant stimulation, and if women could see what men have to do in a gay bathhouse to keep their erections... I mean, it's kind of funny...here you have naked men, beautiful men, some with huge cocks, all gay or bisexual, walking around naked in the steam rooms or the dark rooms or the corridors, and they all have to stroke themselves constantly to keep their erections! I mean, even with all these naked gay men in the most erotic and sexual of all places, they still have to constantly masturbate themselves in order to stay hard. In the gay bathhouse, that's normal... it's understood... it's accepted... but when a man and a woman get together, she expects him to get hard and stay hard without some kind of constant stimulation to his cock! No wonder so many men just fuck women the minute they get hard... they're afraid that they'll lose their erection... If women understood that erections need constant stimulation to stay hard... well... I don't want to get into the politics of sex...

Anyway, Ricardo showered, placed a cock ring around his cock and balls, and started walking around. He started with the steam room... that was his custom because he liked the steam and the dark corners... I don't know what it is about steam that is sexy, but it is... You put of bunch of gay men in a dry sauna, and they just sit there. You put those same gay men in a steam room, with the exact same temperature, and they all start grabbing each other's cocks. It's just the way it is. So Ricardo started off in the steam room You may recall that the steam room at the Primitivo is a bit different that most gay steam rooms—there are very few places to sit. So the men all stand in the darkest corner, towels over their shoulders, stroking themselves, waiting until enough men wander into the steam room. There is some sort of critical mass that happens in a steam room, a certain mathematical event, when enough naked men with erections are just standing next to each other, as more and more men come in, and the group crowds together, there is some sort of unconscious group decision that happens all at once and everyone just starts touching each other. Then someone gets down on their knees and starts blowing someone else and then the group orgy is on. Of course, sexual behavior in gay bathhouses has changed a lot since the coming of AIDS—now most of the men practice safe sex, usually masturbating each other to orgasm, occasionally sucking each other, but the mass amount of barebacking that used to happen in the seventies is just gone.

Anyway, Ricardo went into the steam room and there were a few men standing in the corner, and he joined them, leaning against the wall, stroking himself just like the other men were doing. And in a few minutes some more men came in, and then a few more, and it was starting to get a little crowded, but there were still not enough men. Then one or two more came in, and someone reached over and touched someone else's cock, and then, as if that was a signal, the men started moving in closer as a group. Ricardo reached over to the man to his left and softly stroked his nipple. Someone reached over and started feeling Ricardo's cock, which freed up Ricardo's right hand so that he could reach over and start masturbating some other man's cock. Then someone softly started caressing Ricardo's ass, and then everyone was touching everyone, silently, lovingly, there in the semi-darkness while the steam softly hissed all around them. This went on for several minutes, everyone feeling all the people around them. The point, as you know, is *not* to cum, but to increase the sexual excitement, to stretch out the sex play as long as possible, constantly building the sexual excitement and pleasure until at some point you just can't stand it anymore. It's a shame that no one ever explains all this to straight people— they all have such quick sex, like bunny rabbits—I think only gay men and lesbians really know how to have sex...

And so Ricardo is standing in this group, touching, being touched, and at some point someone gets behind him and reaches both hands around him and begins to massage his nipples. And Ricardo leans back into this man, and the man is a little taller than Ricardo, and so Ricardo is leaning back onto this man's chest. And Ricardo reaches around behind him, under the man's towel, and starts to play with the man's cock. And it's a nice size cock—not too big, but responsive—it just feels like the right size. And the man pulls Ricardo closer to him, and reaches down with one hand and starts playing with Ricardo's cock, and Ricardo leans more into the man, and it feels good, and then the man whispers to Ricardo, asking him in Spanish if he'd like to go to one of the private rooms, and Ricardo says no, but continues to touch the man, and feels a certain comfort, a certain strength from this man's body, and he turns around and looks at the man and he likes what he sees, and the man continues to touch Ricardo, in a soft, gentle way, and so Ricardo finally says, "okay, yes, for just a few minutes, and only with safe play" and the man nods his head and then the man leads the way out of the steam room, with Ricardo following. And they walk through the twisting corridors until they find an empty room, and they both step inside, and Ricardo closes the door.

These rooms, I'm sure you know, just have a plastic covered pad about three feet off the floor on a bed frame. There is a paper towel dispenser on the wall next to some hooks. Ricardo hangs his towel on one hook, and the man hangs his towel on another hook and they both lay down into each other's arms and continue touching and caressing each other.

And I suppose I should say something about Ricardo's personal policy and practice regarding oral sex. As a rule, he never performed oral sex on strangers, but of course he didn't mind if they blew him. Now that wasn't because of HIV. As I'm sure you know, it is almost impossible to catch HIV from oral sex, even if the man cums in your mouth, unless you had some type of open cut or sore in your mouth. By the way, my friend, since we are talking so honestly and openly, may I enquire as to your HIV status? Negative? Good. Me too. I get tested twice a year just to be sure. And you? Yes, that's very prudent. Anyway, Ricardo was HIV negative as well, and planned on keeping it that way. No, the problem with performing oral sex in bathhouses is not STDs—it's TB. No, it's true. If you blow someone's cock, and the fellow before you who had that same cock in his mouth had tuberculosis, you can be exposed to those TB germs from the other man's saliva. Now, this is not as much of a risk as it was a few years ago, before Truvada. Before the Truvada drugs, there were many HIV positive men in the bathhouses who had TB. No so much anymore, but it's still a risk. Of course, if the man has gonorrhea or syphilis, it's possible to catch that from oral sex as well. So as a rule, Ricardo didn't blow men at bathhouses.

That's not to say that Ricardo didn't like giving oral sex. He loved it. That's one of the many advantages of being gay, you know, being able to take another man's cock into your mouth and suck it. I feel sorry for women, because they don't get to see a man's cock until they're in the bedroom, until, in a sense, they've already committed to having sex. Gay men get to go to bathhouses and look at and feel and play with everyone's cock until they find one they like, and then they can suck it. Being gay means you can "try before you buy." Ha. Do you know how many women finally get a man into bed only to be disappointed by the shape or size of the man's cock? I bet it's like fifty percent. Actually, it must be higher. I bet that maybe all women have that experience at some point in their lives. No wonder so many women are bitter.

But I was saying... Ricardo liked giving oral sex. He used to be in a relationship in Panama, years ago, with a young man named Marco. And Ricardo loved blowing Marco and having Marco cum in his mouth. But of course, the reason he loved it so much was that he loved Marco... Marco was a bit shy, and Ricardo would engage in a bit of aggressive sex play, where he would hold Marco down and blow him and Marco would playfully protest, and Ricardo would suck him until Marco moaned and came and then Ricardo would swallow the cum. But again, that was because he loved Marco, and they were in a relationship, and they had both been tested. And that was years ago. So... even though Ricardo liked giving blowjobs, as a rule he never did it in bathhouse... as a rule... of course, sometimes he bent that rule a bit. He never ever let someone cum in his mouth, but if he liked someone that he had met in a bathhouse...if he felt they were safe... he felt that he could trust them... and if the circumstances were right, he would occasionally blow them... never to orgasm, of course. What made him feel safe? Well, take this man I was just telling you about in the steam room. When he first came up behind Ricardo, he still had his towel wrapped around his waist, because he had just came into the steam room, and Ricardo could feel that the man's cock was dry, so he hadn't just been blown by someone else. And the man was respectful towards Ricardo, and they chatted a bit on the way to the private room, and introduced themselves to each other, and the man, whose name was Adolpho, seemed intelligent... but mostly it was a feeling, I guess. So anyway, they lay there together cuddling and touching, playing with each other's cock, grasping each other's asses, and at some point, Ricardo went down and started sucking on Adolpho's cock. After a bit he stopped and then Adolpho went down on Ricardo. And this playing and touching went on for some time, kissing nipples and necks, but not on the mouth, and sucking each other's cocks... They probably spent about thirty minutes in that room doing that, just enjoying each other's bodies and slowly ratcheting up the sexual excitement but never losing control... And then after a while they stopped and just talked a bit, and then it was time to say goodbye and return to the steam room or the dark rooms or whatever.

That's the great thing about bathhouses—you can be completely open and honest and just do exactly what you want—and that's why Ricardo loved them more than any other place or way of meeting other like-minded people. Any other method of meeting requires talking, posturing, and pretending… Only in the bathhouse is sexuality pure and uncontaminated by any type of presentation of self, or any type of status or pretense. You don't have to be clever or witty or wealthy or smart or even good-looking in a bathhouse. Bathhouses are the purest form of democracy that there is.

But that's not to say that one escapes who one is. One never escapes one's own karma, one's own self, even in the anonymous dark steamy corridors of the bathhouse. For example, that evening, after playing with Adolpho, Ricardo spent probably several more hours there, roaming through the labyrinth of dark hallways, dark rooms, video rooms, and of course the steam room. He took a break at one point and had a beer at the bar in the center of the bathhouse and chatted with several men there. And then he returned to his cruising. At one point, he spotted a very slight young Asian man, probably no more than twenty years old. Ricardo's experience with young Asian men in bathhouses, especially if they are slight of build or effeminate, is that they are bottoms. But as he approached this young man, he saw that he was wearing a condom. Now it was possible that the young man was just being extra careful… but it was also possible that he was a top. Ricardo had never seen a slight Asian man act like a top, and the thought of it excited him. He wondered what it would be like to be fucked by this slight effeminate man, but the Asian man moved away as Ricardo approached and disappeared into the darkness. So Ricardo walked down another corridor and continued with his cruising. At one point he came upon a private room with the door open, and there was a larger man lying there on his stomach wearing a pair of woman's panties. Ricardo thought back to Marilyn, and for a brief second the question crossed his mind why he was so attracted to transvestites. He stepped into the room, but didn't close the door. The man didn't even look up to see who had entered the room, but just spread his legs a little and arched his ass just a little into the air. Ricardo reached down and felt the man's ass though his panties, felt the lace that covered the man's ass, then he reached down further underneath the man's ass where the panties hugged the man's balls, and Ricardo played with them for a while. He felt himself getting hard, and he wondered what it would be like to fuck this man's ass. So he walked out of the private room, and went down the hall to where on the wall there was a small metal box like a trough that held condoms and small packets of lubricants. Ricardo grabbed one of each and then walked back to the private room. But when he got there, he saw that another man had entered, had pulled down the man's panties and was actively rimming the man. So Ricardo returned to the metal trough and put the condom and the packet of lubricant back.

Anyway, the point I was trying to make about karma, is that all of this cruising went on for several hours, and the sexual excitement in Ricardo was building up to the point that now he wanted to cum. So he went into the largest darkroom where a group of men had gathered. Here there were benches and low beds built into the walls and several couples were fucking on the beds and several men were sitting next on the benches while other men kneeled in front of them, blowing them. A group of men had gathered around one such couple and the group of men were all touching each other. Ricardo moved towards that group, stroking himself. The men were standing in a small circle, like a wagon train circled to protect itself. Ricardo could see two young men in the center on their knees blowing two of the men who were standing. Ricardo ran his hand gently over the ass of one of the men standing there, but the man pushed his hand away. Another man moved away as Ricardo approached him. There was a third man stroking his cock nearby, and Ricardo moved closer to him, hoping to feel his cock, but he moved away as well. Everyone in the group seemed to be getting all equally as excited as Ricardo. He could hear one of the men on the nearby bed who was being fucked in the ass start to moan loudly, as the man behind him rammed him harder and harder. One of the men in the center of the circle who was being blown began to moan. Ricardo continued to stroke himself and felt himself starting to lose control. He reached over to another man and touched his chest and then started to run his hand down the man's front to his cock when the man pulled away. Ricardo stepped over to another old man who was holding a rather large cock but that man moved away too. Finally the excitement was more than Ricardo could stand and he felt himself starting to cum. He was standing beside one of the low beds so he aimed his cock under the bed frame and squirted hot cum onto the floor away from where anyone would step on it. He came hard and it was good, but at the same time, there he was, masturbating himself to orgasm while all around him, just inches away, all the other gay men were touching each other, or being touched by someone else. There he was in the midst of this orgy of cocks being handled, squeezed, stroked, and sucked, and he was masturbating himself to orgasm alone. See what I mean about karma? The irony didn't escape Ricardo either. After he came, he rested a bit, leaning on the wall, and breathing heavily. And then he went and showered, got dressed, and walked back to his hotel.

Chapter 8: Calle de la Montera

The next night, Ricardo tried a different approach. His hotel, as I've mentioned, was near the Calle de la Montera. Ah, I see you know that area. Well, he decided that maybe he would try his luck with women again. So he sat at one of the many outdoor cafés there on that street and had some wine and something to eat, and just watched the prostitutes work the street. Now, that street, as you know, is famous for prostitutes. But do you know why? It's because about ten years or so ago, the Russian economy was in the upswing part of their boom-bust economy, and many Russian entrepreneurs who had gotten rich quickly started buying buildings throughout Europe, as a way of moving money out of Russia... you know, to secure their wealth before the economy went bust again. And some of these Russians bought several buildings on or near the Calle de la Montera in Madrid, and they bought them through some Eastern European mafia types to conceal who the real owners were, and they let these Eastern European thugs manage the buildings, and those Eastern Europeans turned the buildings into brothels as a way of making them profitable for themselves. Yes, yes, I know... I understand... Prostitution is legal in Spain but brothels are not. Well, let me explain. These Russians set up dummy corporations and leased the buildings to their Eastern European friends, mostly from Hungary, and the Hungarians then brought women over to live in the buildings and work as prostitutes. Now, there was no trickery involved here with these women... they weren't told they would be working in restaurants or anything... they knew they were coming here to be sex workers, and they came willingly...well, I guess "willingly" is a conditional word... insomuch as they understood that they could make more money in Spain as prostitutes than they ever could earn doing whatever in Hungary... so they came to Spain "voluntarily" so to speak, and their Hungarian landlords rented them a room in these buildings on or near the Calle de la Montera and the women would take their clients there. Well, when I say they rented them a room, I mean that they had them sign a lease that said they were renting a room, so it looked on paper like they were independent women. But in essence it was a brothel, because there were maybe twenty or thirty women living in these apartments, and they had to pay their Hungarian landlords more than the rent in the written lease, but the women did get to keep a certain percent. So they worked hard, standing on the corners of the Calle de la Montera, beckoning to lonely tourists, all those men who walked that street on their way to the famous Puerta del Sol nearby.

Anyway, Ricardo didn't know about the economics of these Hungarian women. He didn't even know most of them were Hungarian—he only knew the street was famous for prostitutes. So that night, as I've mentioned, he positioned himself at one of the outdoor cafés and had some wine and watched the hookers work. As I say, he thought they were independent workers, like how it is in Amsterdam... he didn't understand that there was a mafia-like enterprise behind the hookers. So he watched, as he drank his wine and ate his tapas dinner, he watched them interact with whatever men approached them.

He saw how the young men would approach them and flirt with them, and how the women would laugh, but turn them down... It was because the young men didn't have money, you know, at least not enough money for these girls... And he noticed that after any man left the women without consummating a deal, an older woman would emerge from the shadows and talk with the woman. So it didn't take Ricardo long to figure out that this older woman was managing the prostitutes... managing in the sense of asking them why they hadn't been able to consummate a deal with whatever man had approached them. And it made Ricardo curious, you know, since these women were supposed to be independent, why some older manager would suddenly appear and talk to each of them whenever they hadn't been able to "make a sale", so to speak. And so, after he had had several glasses of wine to screw up his courage, he paid his bill and went up and talked to one of the women. Now, talking with a prostitute is a bit like making small talk with a loan shark—you're only allowed so much small talk until you need to come to the point. So Ricardo would pretend to get to the point very quickly and then make small talk while he pretended to be considering the deal. "How much?" would be his leading question, and they would quote a price, and he'd furrow his brow and nod his head as if he was thinking about it, and then he would ask them what their name was—even though he knew they weren't using their real names—and where they were from. Then he would say something like "let me think about it for a minute" and he'd wander off, just down the avenue, until he came to another hooker, and then he'd ask the same questions... and what he discovered intrigued him. First, all of the prices were exactly the same, and the patter was exactly the same: "Fifty Euros fuck or suck" was what each girl told him, the exact same phrase, and when he asked where they were from, it was always Hungary... and if he asked if they would come to his hotel, they always said no, that they had their own place on the next block, and they all had the same patter—that the place was safe and they could go there and have sex. And after talking to about ten of these pavement princesses on the Calle de la Montera that night, always getting the same answer, Ricardo pretty much had it figured out. They all pointed to the same direction when they referred to "their place" which they called "their apartment" but they kept referring to having a room there, so he figured out pretty quick that they all lived in the same place, and they were all being managed by some older people. And it made him sad... because he really liked prostitutes, but he hated the exploitation of prostitutes, and he figured that whenever someone was "managing" them, they were being exploited. He much preferred the Amsterdam system, where each hooker was licensed and regulated, and where she was a true independent, renting a window in the red light district, rather than the Spanish system, where prostitution simply wasn't illegal, and no one was licensed, no one had health inspections, and no one really checked up on whether these women were being exploited or not.

So, of course, he did not take any of those girls' offers that night, even though many of them were young and beautiful. He didn't want to be led to their "apartment"... he didn't want to meet whatever thug was protecting them at the apartment... he just didn't want any part of that system.

But fortunately, he had a backup plan. Remember what I said about his preference for Asian prostitutes? Well, he was hoping the Thai Palace was still open. The Thai Palace was not really Thai and it certainly wasn't a palace, and it wasn't quite a brothel, but damn close. It was a massage joint, staffed mostly by Malaysian women, none particularly young, but all actually authentic masseuses. They did legitimate foot massages in the front area by a large window where the public could see how "legitimate" they were, and they did back and shoulder massages in the back. Now they wouldn't tell you this up front, but if you asked to go upstairs you could get a full body massage with either a "happy ending" or actual sex.

Now to me, I don't know what the difference is between the girls on the Calle de la Montera and these Asian masseuses. To me it seems like the same setup. But somehow, Ricardo saw it differently. Maybe it was because the Asian women there always seemed happy and relaxed, and didn't have that haunted look in their eyes that those gaunt Hungarian women on the street had. I don't know. Or maybe he had been there enough times over the years to reassure himself that the women weren't being exploited... Or maybe he just wanted to believe that so he could relax and enjoy himself. But whatever the truth was, he headed over there that night, went inside and asked for a full one-hour massage upstairs with all the trimmings, as it were.

Now I will say, that if one is going to pay for sex, then having a full massage before the sex is the way to go. The skin trade is just not what it used to be in Europe. As I mentioned, when Ricardo was a young man living in Spain and going to prostitutes, there were caresses and kisses. He was never rushed, and he would leave the place feeling loved. But that was then. Nowadays, prostitution in Europe is just like McDonalds—you get in, place your order, pay your money, and gobble down your McBlowJob and you're done in ten or fifteen minutes and back outside. So the massage joints are the only place left in Europe where you actually count on getting to relax and being touched before sex.

Now I'm just talking about Europe here. The prostitutes that Ricardo knew in Panama were not like that. But then again, he was a regular at those Panamanian brothels, so he was treated better.

Anyway, he headed over to the Thai Palace that night. The downstairs was full of weary tourists getting foot massages. But of course Ricardo asked to go upstairs. The older woman whom he spoke to looked at him for a moment, and then said, "You been here before?" And Ricardo nodded. Then she said, "You want full service?" And again he nodded. Then she nodded and led him through a hallway to a winding staircase that led upwards. At the foot of the staircase she simply said, "You go room two", and then she walked away. Ricardo climbed up the steep winding staircase to the next floor, found room number two, and went inside. Inside he found a large bed, with a large fresh towel spread out over the mid-portion of the bed, a dresser with mirror, a small table with bottles of massage oil and a paper towel dispenser, and a bathroom complete with shower. The place was clean and orderly.

One of the differences between a massage joint and a brothel is that you don't get to pick your prostitute in a massage joint. You simply get told which room to go to, and the madam will send in whatever masseuse happenes to be available. You might get a young pretty woman or an older woman. I don't know why it's that way, but in any massage joint that's how it is. I suppose it's a way of saving face, of keeping up the appearance of a legitimate business. After all, you're paying for the massage skill for your tired muscles, not for the girl. And for Ricardo, it made those places kind of fun—it was like a sexual grab bag. You never knew what, or in this case, *who*, you were going to get. But you always got a good massage. Ha, Ricardo had fucked some pretty old women at massage joints over the years. But this time he was lucky. The woman who came up to his room was young—young by massage joint standards. She was between thirty and forty, Ricardo guessed. And he found her attractive. He was sitting on the bed when she came in. She was wearing a black slip and halter top and carrying their "menu" of services, which he handed to him. It was a printed cardboard page that listed the prices for each act, rather like a dim sum menu in several languages: 50 Euros for a 30-minute massage with happy ending, i.e. handjob; or 80 Euros for a 60 minute massage with a happy ending; and then you could add on the "extras" to the massage: 30 Euros for a blowjob, or 40 Euros for actual fucking. And the menu had large printing at the bottom indicating that all the women were independent workers. Ricardo just pointed to the option that indicated an hour massage followed by fucking.

"You pay now," she said, and Ricardo handed her 120 Euros. She said, "You take off clothes and lie face down." Ricardo did as he was told, while the woman left the room to take the money downstairs.

When she returned a few minutes later, Ricardo was naked and lying down on the bed as told. She disappeared into the bathroom.

He heard her washing her hands, and then she came back into the room, he turned his head and upper body and looked at her. She was taking off her halter top and slip, but she left her panties on. Ricardo liked what he saw—small breasts with tiny dark nipples.

"Where are you from?" he asked her in Spanish.

"From Thailand," she responded.

This, of course, was unusual. Most of the women who worked there were from Malaysia or the Philippines.

Now Ricardo didn't speak Thai, of course, but he knew a few phrases in Lao, which is close to Thai, so he said, "Sa-bai-dee", and she smiled and replied, "Sa-bai-dee-mai" and put her hands together in the traditional little prayer bow to him, and then added in Spanish, "You speak Thai?"

Ricardo put his hands together, as best he could since he was lying naked face down on the bed, but he returned the gesture of respect to her, and said, "No, just enough to say hello."

"Where you learn?" she asked.

"I had friends from Laos, years ago," he said, and then asked, "What's your name?"

"Mee," she replied as she reached for the bottle of massage oil. She poured some oil into her hand and rubbed it a bit to warm it up and then started working on Ricardo's back.

They chatted for a little bit, but soon her touch started to relax him, and he shut up and just let her work. As I said, all of the women who worked there were trained masseuses, and Mee gave him a good massage: she pressed hard into the muscles of his shoulders and back, worked down his legs, massaged the soles of his feet, taking her time. The part he liked the best though was when she massaged his buttocks. She was straddling his lower body as she did this, and Ricardo could feel her muscular thighs gripping his upper legs as she leaned into the massage. Yes, if you're going to pay for sex, getting a massage first is the only way to go.

Eventually she told him to turn over, worked on his chest a bit, then stood up and removed her black panties.

"You want suck?" she asked.

He shook his head no. "Just fuck," he said.

She nodded and grabbed a condom from the table, opened it and rolled it over his semi-hard cock. Then she simply masturbated him until he got harder, squirted some lubricant from a tube over his cock, and then straddled him and slid him inside her.

Now, as I've said before, most prostitutes like to be

on top because they can control the pressure, the rhythm, and the speed of the fucking, and they almost always sit straight up, on top of the man, using their thighs to raise and lower themselves up and down over his cock. But Mee leaned completely forward, lying on top of Ricardo, wrapping her arms around him and allowing him to wrap his arms around her, while keeping her knees bent and using her thighs to pump just her pelvis up and down, slowly at first, and then faster and faster, holding him tightly. Ricardo found this extremely erotic. He began to moan softly, and she ground her pelvis into his, forcing his cock deep inside her. It was good, and Ricardo came. She held him tightly while he came and his arms spasmed a bit. Then she climbed off him, and handed him several paper towels. He removed the condom, wiped his cock, and tossed the paper towels into the small trash can.

"That was good, Mee. Thank you," he said.

"You want shower?" she asked, pointed to the bathroom.

"No, no, I'm okay," he said knowing his hotel was only a short walk away and that he would shower there.

"Okay," she said. "I shower now. You find your way downstairs." And she disappeared into the bathroom. He heard the shower come on.

Ricardo slowly put his clothes back on, left a thirty-Euro tip on the bed, and carefully navigated the spiral staircase down to the first floor and then walked out the front door into the evening.

He was walking on the Gran Via, that wide sidewalk lined with stores and full of people, but he was oblivious to everything and everyone. His mind was empty. That's the thing about good sex, you know—it wipes away all thought and worries. Maybe that's why Phillipe had recommended that Ricardo embrace sex— she knew that he needed to have his mind washed clean. People were walking and talking all around him, but he was only aware of his own body, moving step by step back to the hotel. He passed where the Gran Via intersects the Calle de la Montera, and he glanced down the street. The Hungarian hookers were still standing in a small group underneath the trees. But they no longer interested him. He walked back to his hotel.

Chapter 9: Connecting the Dots

I've been telling you all these things in an attempt to strip away all pretence, to try and describe life as it really is—Ricardo's life—which, I suppose, is everyone's life. It's just that it's so much easier to strip away the façade with Ricardo. He had done half the work himself over his decades of living, just letting those attributes of society fall to the wayside, moving to Panama where no one cared who he was or what he had accomplished, and thus he no longer needed to present himself to anyone, he no longer needed an identity... And then, of course, life had done the other half—wearing his granite viewpoints down like soft sandstone, washing away all his friends one by one... all those landmarks of people that we use to navigate our way through life—they're like lighthouses in our lives, keeping us on track, reminding us who we are and where we're going, and once they're gone, the outline of the coast becomes vague, indistinct, and foreign to us, and we begin to drift... And of course there was that strange addiction he had to writing... Ha! He used to say that it was the process of writing that bleached his soul—that after a day of sitting at a desk and pouring words onto his laptop computer screen, his soul felt like an old bleached whalebone exposed on the shore for the world to see, to walk by and look at, and then to walk away from. I don't know. He liked to talk a lot, but *my* purpose, my purpose here is to describe this man to you and to explain how he ended up on that airport floor with María.

By the way, how was your dinner? Good, eh? I tell you, this little bar is a hidden gem in this town. Don't tell anyone about it. The last thing I want here is word getting out about how good this place is. Would you like some dessert? No, I'm full too, but I guarantee you the owner will present us with a small plate of cheese in a bit. But in the meantime, let's just enjoy this wine and I'll tell you about Ricardo's last evening in Madrid.

The morning after his visit to the Thai Palace, he decided that it was time to make plans to get to Barcelona. It's really takes about the same travel time to fly or take the high-speed train from Madrid to Barcelona. But for some reason, Ricardo decided to fly, and so he booked a flight for the next afternoon. Then he turned his attention to deciding what he wanted to do for his last night in Madrid.

He thought over his previous week's experiences in Amsterdam and Madrid, considering what he had liked and what hadn't pleased him as much. Even though he liked the Primitivo bathhouse, his experience there his first night in Madrid had left him feeling rather lonely, so he decided not to go back there. Maybe it's man's need for variety, or maybe it was just his need for variety of perversity. But Ricardo decided that that he wanted to try one of those sex clubs that he mentioned to Phillipe so many weeks earlier. He knew of the ones in Berlin, of course—they were famous—but he didn't know if there were any in Madrid, so he spent his morning on the internet researching this.

Now, when I say sex club, I'm talking those clubs that couples belong to—what used to be called swingers' clubs. Ever been to one? No? Well, sex clubs are, by nature, hard to find. They evolved out of the wife-swapping and swinger scene in the sixties, but they're not like other sex businesses. All other sex businesses want clients from off the street. But the sex clubs exist to serve their paying members, who are all couples, so they only need more couples, or single bisexual females, and only occasionally—rarely—do they need single men. The ones in Berlin are different, because the "couples" in those clubs are actually employees, so the men customers are actually paying for an orgy with male and female prostitutes. Those are basically brothels dressed up to look like swingers' clubs and they advertise and promote themselves heavily to tourists. But real sex clubs are hard to find. They don't advertise. Ricardo was only able to find one in Madrid, a place in an upscale part of the Salamanca area. I'm sure there are more swingers' clubs in Madrid, but they are hidden, and he could only find a reference to that one. It wasn't close to his hotel, but it was walkable, maybe a thirty or forty minute walk. It was simply called "Nuestro Lugar", or Our Place. They didn't have a website, but he found a mention of them in some online review of sex establishments, and from there he tracked down their Facebook page, and there he found a calendar of upcoming events. They were scheduled to open their doors at nine p.m. for a "bi" party. Members got in free, as well as any unattached females. Single males had to pay a twenty Euro cover and there was a two-drink minimum. The dress code was listed as "sexy black" and it was evident that there would be a bouncer at the door to decide who got in and who didn't. Ricardo didn't think his chances were great but he figured, why not try? He had a black t-shirt and a black jacket that looked pretty good with jeans, so that night he put them on and headed over there. He waited until ten to leave his hotel, because he knew that partying in Madrid really doesn't start until midnight, but he had given up staying out to the wee hours of the morning many years ago. He was only hoping that he might find some couple there early who would be interested in fucking him

You know, the nature of illusion is interesting. It's like being half asleep, where you are aware that you are dreaming, and yet it's pleasant, and so you lay there and continue to dream, and continue to watch yourself dream. I think we maintain our illusions the same way. We *know* they are illusions, but they are so pleasant that we sleepwalk through the day just watching them unfold. When Ricardo told me all this, months after it all happened, he explained that he knew he was going to be rejected at the door of the place. No matter how well he dressed, he knew how he looked—I mean, he can still pass for maybe as young as 60, maybe 58 on a really good day, but that's as good as it gets for him. His beard is almost white, and, well, there is just something about age that always shows—the shape of the body, the extra fold of skin on the neck, the way of moving. Ricardo could have dressed up in as flashy of a sexy black outfit as he wanted, but he still looked like an older man, or a middle-aged man at best. And he knew this. He knew he would never get past the bouncer. And yet he went anyway. He was hoping that luck would help him. He walked the forty minutes to the address, knocked on the door and a bouncer of some sort opened it and talked to him for a bit. The bouncer was polite, but told him that they had enough single guys there already and that he should try and come back in a couple of hours, which Ricardo felt was code for *don't come back at all* because Ricardo could tell the man was lying. But on some level, it just didn't surprise Ricardo, so he nodded and left. The disappointment was not crushing, because, as I said, he knew it was going to happen. But it did leave him feeling rather flat. He told himself that he should have hired some escort off of Craigslist, or maybe one of those Hungarian hookers, to accompany him, to pretend to be a couple, so he would have gotten right into that club. But he knew he didn't have the energy for that level of organized effort.

But he did have a plan B. That's one of the advantages of being older, you know—always having a contingency plan. His plan B was to walk to La Lunita, a small tranny bar in the Chueca District, not far from his hotel. He remembered it from years ago, and so, before he left his hotel to walk to Nuestro Lugar, he looked up La Lunita online to make sure it was still open. La Lunita is actually kind of an odd place—it's not really correct to call it a tranny bar—it's just that all the male staff dress up in these fabulous dresses, so it has the feel of a tranny bar, but it's really more of a dance bar with a dance floor in the basement and a bar on the first floor. The bartenders and waiters flirt around in leather dresses or long evening gowns upstairs serving drinks and making chit-chat, and occasionally bursting into song. Lots of women, gay and straight, come there to dance and usually head straight downstairs where there is a large dance floor, a beer bar, and pulsating dance music. But the soundproofing is good, and upstairs was where Ricardo used to hang out years ago. La Lunita has been through a series of owners but its character and theme has remained constant. Back when Ricardo was in his twenties and living in Madrid... and we're talking a few centuries ago, ha!...he could always count on being able to come to La Lunita to find some handsome lad to take home, or an occasional tranny, and once in a great while, even a young woman.

And the place looked the same from the outside as he approached it that evening. A few trannies were standing on the sidewalk out in front having a cigarette and talking loudly. Music and colored lights from inside the bar poured out into the street. There was a sound and feel of festivity about the entrance. People were going in and out. Unlike a lot of gay bars even in the Chueca District, La Lunita didn't hide behind a solid front wall with a solid door. To the contrary, the bar had huge glass windows so that everyone could see the people inside. There was nothing shy or demure about La Lunita. Ricardo liked that about the place.

He walked inside and made his way up to the bar and ordered a glass of white wine. Once he got his drink, and after admiring the bartender in a white leather bustier, Ricardo moved away from the mirrored bar and luckily found an empty seat next to the side wall. He sat there and sipped his wine and surveyed the scene. His first impression was that that the place had been frozen in time for the last 40 years: There was the same crowded bar, loud music, people waving and shouting and smiling, stylish clothes and stylish haircuts. The music was different; the haircuts were different; the clothes were different; and yet it all still felt so stylish, so avant-garde. He took a moment to admire how handsome the young men and the young women were. Everyone was swirling, moving about, trying to get to the back to go downstairs and dance, or trying to get to the bar to get a drink, or trying to get outside for a smoke. There was just this flow of color and movement, and young, young bodies, like a river of fashionably-clothed flesh, muscular arms on the boys and on the trannies and on some of the girls, and cleavage, real or otherwise, on boys and girls. But most of all energy, youthful energy, all swirling around him. The energy was contagious, and he felt transfixed by the glitter, the make-up, the flesh, and the constant movement. Everyone seemed so beautiful.

It was then, as he was surveying this river of beautiful flesh swirling all around him, that he looked up and caught a glimpse of his reflection in the bar mirror across from where he was sitting, and somehow the reflection and the light on his face made the whiteness of his beard even whiter, or maybe it was the black shirt and jacket he was wearing that contrasted with—and amped up—the amount of white in his beard and hair, so that his cheeks and eyes and forehead seemed enveloped and lit up by white phosphorus, and in that single image he realized what he must look like to everyone else there, and he realized not only was he the oldest person in that bar, but that there was no one there even close to his age, and he realized then why no one was making eye contact with him as they swirled around him—it was *because* he was the oldest person there, way older than all of them, and thus he was totally and utterly invisible to them. The sea of youthful flesh that two minutes before had been so beautiful to him was also completely oblivious to him. They were programmed by their youth to immediately ignore him, to dismiss him, to not even see him. It was a beautiful river alright, but not one he could touch, and not one that would touch him, and in that moment he remembered a fragment of that dream of a vast river he had had the night after going to Jimmy's bathhouse in New York, except in that dream the bodies were all dead and bloated, and here they were all alive and svelte. Nonetheless the image disturbed him, and so he left his wine glass, still half-full, on the side bar and walked outside.

The blast of cool night air outside seemed to prop him up as he walked away. He found himself just walking, walking in the general direction back towards his hotel. He didn't have a plan C. The rejection he had felt at Nuestro Lugar had left him feeling a bit disappointed. But the experience of seeing himself in the mirror behind the bar at La Lunita, that old face sitting there like death among all those fabulous young stylish faces, well, that had left his soul feeling really bad, almost numb.

It's like I said last night—sometimes the process of connecting the dots is simply seeing the dots that have always been there right in front of you, staring you in the face. When he was back in Panama, before going to New York, Ricardo thought he was just feeling out of sorts, weary, irritable. He thought he just needed a change of scenery. He hadn't realized that he was grieving... grieving for something he would never have again... that his soul had begun to despair because he had gotten old and no longer had love in his life. He was entering his final block of time on earth and all he had left in Panama for companions were either prostitutes in brothels or the groping of other anonymous old men in the dark steam rooms of the gay bathhouses. His soul knew it, but it hadn't sunk into his consciousness until that moment that that was all he had left... You know, when you're young, you always think that love can come your way... you can structure long periods of alone time without love, because you believe love will come eventually... but sometimes it just doesn't... sometimes it just doesn't. And these thoughts—these dots—were connecting themselves as Ricardo walked through the streets of Madrid that night.

And he just walked around. He walked past his hotel. He walked up the Gran Via past the intersection where the Calle de la Montera begins. He could see the Hungarian hookers standing gaunt under the trees, smoking their cigarettes. He walked farther. He thought he was just walking aimlessly, but he knew where his feet were taking him. Just ten blocks more down the Gran Via, down a side street four blocks or so, away from the lights and traffic, and there he was... standing in front of the Primitivo Bathhouse. He stood there on the sidewalk, just staring at the little metal sign on the door. PRIMITIVO. He thought about that word for a minute, and about his life. If anonymous sex was all that life had left to offer him, he thought, why not embrace it? Why not accept it? I mean, how many years did he have left? Five? Ten? Fifteen, tops? How many years could he count on even being able to get around? It only took him a blink of an eye to get to be as old has he was—another microsecond more and he would be 75, and then 80... if he even lived that long. He could hear a voice softly rationalizing his entire future... Why fight it? Just accept that for his remaining years love would consist of sitting in a pitch-black steam room sucking on an anonymous cock, or two, or three. What did it matter? Why not let them cum in his mouth? Why not lie there face down in the tiny rooms of the bathhouse, his ass all lubed up for whatever man wanted to fuck him? What was the point of trying to find a woman now? He was simply too old, out of the running, over the hill, and out of luck. If not the gay bathhouses, then what else remained opened for him? Where else could he go for love? For sex?

A few men walked past him as he stood there thinking, and they glanced at him as they went into the door. Ricardo took a deep breath of air. He looked up at the stars. Maybe the bathhouse was all that was available to him, but he just didn't feel like it that night. The idea of naked men standing around stroking their cocks, grabbing his cock, or playing with his ass, simply didn't hold any appeal for him that evening. He turned around and walked back to his hotel.

...Ah! A cheese plate. *Quelle surprise! Monsieur, vous* êtes *trop bon, je vous remercie. Merci beaucoup!*...

Actually, to be honest, he brings it by every night I eat here, but I always act surprised. And it's pretty good cheese. Try a piece. See? Yes, it's quite good, isn't it?

...Well, my young friend, there is only one last part of my story left, but once again, I have talked too much, and our dinner is over and the wine appears to be gone. Perhaps you would care to come to my apartment for a nightcap. It's not a far walk from here, and I think you might be interested in some of my artifacts, and I can tell you what happened to Ricardo at the airport the following day. You have time? Ah, good.

Chapter 10: Airport

What a pleasant evening. I love this city this time of year. In a few weeks a scarf and hat will be required, but right now the freshness of the air is very enjoyable. That was a lovely dinner. Thank you for sharing it with me and allowing me to ramble on so. Oh, you are too kind. Ah yes, well the topic of sexuality interests me, too. Human beings are a strange lot, and there are those among us, and I can tell you are one of them, who know we are different, who manage to appear to fit in, but still have our own ways. Yes, this street, it's not far. As we walk I shall continue... if I can remember where I left off. Let's see... oh, yes... So Ricardo simply went back to the hotel that night feeling rather dead, very flat... well, feeling very old. And he woke up feeling that same way the next morning... that is, feeling old and robotic. He got up, showered and dressed, and packed his backpack in this rather automatic way. He went down to the hotel lobby for coffee and a continental breakfast, and it was then that he realized that it was still quite early, but he didn't care anymore. He figured he might as well check out anyway. He could just as well wait at the airport for a few extra hours as he could sit in a tiny hotel room and wait.

And that's why he ended up getting to the airport early that day. It was just an accident. Oh, you could say it was fate, but I think that he was just depressed and didn't care where he waited, so he caught a cab to the airport and ended up getting there several hours before his flight was scheduled to leave. People always ascribe fate to things that happen, you know—it's human nature. No matter what happens, they say it was fate. Well, we'll never know, will we? I mean, it's not like the fates are going to reveal themselves to us and say "Yoo-hoo, it's us! Be sure to get to the airport early today. We have a surprise for you." Ha. No, I don't think it works that way. What? Oh yes, I do believe there is such a thing as fate, yes indeed, but I just assume it works in some way that is so far above our comprehension that we can never figure it out. Nonetheless, it is true that as Ricardo was getting out of his cab at the airport, he saw María Montagé walking through the crowd on the sidewalk, holding Sophi. So who knows, maybe it was fate.

He could tell she had been crying. Even though she had a bit of make-up on, there was that telltale puffiness around the eyes. But she smiled when he called out to her, and she went up to him. Even though he had only met her that one time before, he leaned forward and gave her the customary Spanish kiss on the cheek, and when he did he caught her scent—whether it was perfume or not, he couldn't tell—but it pleased him.

"I need to find a bathroom for Sophi," María yelled over the traffic noise.

"Come with me," Ricardo said, "I know where the nearest one is."

One of the things about being older, you know, is that you instinctively learn to map out where the bathrooms are when you first arrive at a new location, and Ricardo had automatically done just that a few days earlier when he arrived at the Madrid airport from Amsterdam. So he remembered that there was a small toilet right around the corner from where they were standing. He led María there, and waited outside while she took Sophi inside.

María came out of the toilet holding Sophi a few minutes later, looking a bit less harried. "Thank you, Ricardo. I'm glad you knew where this was. It's so good to see you again."

"It's good to see you too, María," Ricardo said, "but I'm surprised. Are you traveling somewhere? I thought you were going to stay in Madrid."

María looked away, but Ricardo could tell she was fighting to hold back tears. "Things did not work out with Artemio," she said. "I'm going back to California."

"What? Oh Jeez, María... shit, I'm sorry." Ricardo looked at her, took a deep breath, and said, "Look, when is your flight? Do you have time for a cup of coffee?"

"All I have is time, Ricardo. My flight is not until this afternoon. I just had nowhere else to go, so I came here." Tears began to flow down her cheeks. "His mother threw me out. I couldn't believe he wouldn't stand up to her. He is just a little mama's boy. I don't know what I saw in him. I would have left two days ago, but this was the first flight out I could get... well, the first flight out I could afford..."

María stood there holding Sophi and crying. Ricardo took her gently by the arm and said, "There's a little coffee shop inside the terminal, María. Come on."

He walked her inside the terminal, past the check-in counters to a little coffee shop that was located right ahead of where the Security lines began. He sat her down at a corner table, and then went and brought a tray back to the table with an espresso for her, an Americano for him, and a plastic glass of juice for Sophi. María had stopped crying, but her emotions were still raw on her face and aching to come out. All Ricardo had to do is say, "Tell me what happened," and the words began to pour out of her. She told him how Artemio's mother had accused her of being a gold digger, saying that her son was not Sophi's father, and claiming that María was making this all up to steal the family money. She called María a whore and a *zamba*, Spanish slang for half-breed.

"Artemio said nothing during this. Nothing! He wasn't anything like the man I knew back in California."

"Well," Ricardo offered, "you never really know someone until you see them on their home territory, especially young men."

"You know, when I first told him I wanted to come see him and bring Sophi, he seemed excited. But the closer the time came for me to fly here, the more I thought he was acting distant. I just assumed that once I got here, everything would be fine."

"Uh huh," said Ricardo and reflected to himself how he never assumed anything would be fine, but he only said, "What will you do now?"

"I emailed my Dad, to let him know I was coming back. I know he would like to help, but there's not much he can do. He got remarried a few years ago, and his new wife has three kids. I was renting a room in San Diego from a friend. That's where I want to go back to. I emailed her and asked if I could come back. Maybe she hasn't rented the room out yet. I'm hoping I can stay there again, but if not, I have some other friends I can crash with until I find a place to live. I had a job working in a daycare in San Diego, and they let me bring Sophi, and I'm hoping I can get that job back. "

"Have you talked with the daycare place?" Ricardo asked.

"No, I'll call them when I get back to San Diego," María said.

Sophi started to spill her glass of juice and María turned her attention to the child. While she was wiping Sophi's chin and talking to Sophi, Ricardo tried to take stock of the situation. He really didn't know this girl, really knew nothing about her. She was maybe, what? Twenty-eight or thirty years old... working at a daycare so she could get free daycare for Sophi... had been foolish enough to get pregnant by someone who clearly was irresponsible... had spent all her money to travel to Spain based on some magical thinking that Artemio's family would welcome her with open arms and the future would turn out perfect. There was nothing about her story that evinced any worldly knowledge, intelligence, or sophistication. Ricardo remembered that she had told him she met Artemio at some university, but he really didn't even know if she was a college graduate or not. Everything he knew about her story was just one mistake after another... and yet, somehow, watching her talk to Sophi seemed to soften Ricardo. She was so attentive, so loving, so gentle with that child, that surely, he thought, María must be a good person. No matter that her own life was in an uproar, she was smiling and talking to Sophi in the same calm voice that she always used with her. Surely, Ricardo thought, that counts for something in this world.

And for some reason, that last thought made him think of his own life. What had he, with all his education... all his good fortune... and all his good choices—what had he done with his life? Chased whores? Chased trannies? Sought out the darkest corners of gay bathhouses? María was doing more good in these few minutes by paying attention to Sophi, protecting her, caring for her, trying to create a good life for her... than any good Ricardo had ever done.

Maybe it was the bleakness of his own life that motivated him to say what he said next... I don't know... But I like to think it was that undercurrent of kindness that had been building inside him, building and growing deep inside him... but he felt he had to help this woman, that he had to do something. He looked down the large aisle of people beyond the perimeter of the coffee shop—all those people rushing back and forth, all those important people, going somewhere important, rushing, ignoring each other... then he turned to María and said, "María, listen to me. I want to say something important."

María turned her attention from Sophi and looked at Ricardo.

"María, I know you don't know me... but... do you want to come to Panama with me?"

Her eyes widened, and she looked a little afraid.

Ricardo raised both his open palms in protest. "Look," he said, "I promise you, I'm not trying to put the moves on you. I really just want to help. If you want to come to Panama, I can find a place for you to stay. You could take some time to... to get organized, to decide what you want to do..."

"No, no Ricardo, I appreciate that, but no, I want to go home to California."

Ricardo thought how crazy his proposal must have sounded to her. He nodded his head and said, "Okay, okay, I understand, I understand. But I still want to help. I'm going to give you my email and my phone number down in Panama. I promise you that everything is going to be okay. I want you to stay in contact with me. If you can't find a place to live or a job in San Diego, I will send you money to cover you until you do... or... well... or, if you change your mind about Panama, let me know, and I'll send you a ticket... Look, really, I'm not trying to put the moves on you... I'm not trying to get into your pants... really... but it's just that everyone in life hits a wall sometimes; everyone needs a bit of help sometimes. Sometimes these bad things in life happen, and, well... and they're blessings in disguise. Maybe your future with

Sophi is better without Artemio. But the point is, you're going to be okay. I promise you. I can help."

"Oh no, Ricardo, I am not asking…"

"I know you're not asking for my help. I'm just telling you it's there if you need it. Here, let me write down my information…" and Ricardo took out his small notebook from his inside pocket, tore out a page, and wrote down his name, his email, his phone number in Panama, his address in Panama, and Phillipe's name and address and phone number in New York, and handed the piece of paper to María.

"This is my phone number in Panama; this is my email; this is my address in Panama, and this is a friend of mine in New York who always knows where I am and how to get a hold of me. Put this paper in your purse. All I'm asking is that you stay in touch with me when you get to California. Just let me know what you end up doing and if you need anything. Okay? Is that a deal?"

María took the paper, smiled, and said, "It's a deal," then carefully folded the paper and put it in her wallet inside her purse.

"Thank you, Ricardo," she said.

"Well, you're welcome. I know I must sound crazy, but I've lived so long and… well I just think good people need to be helped out, and I think you're a good person. Everything is going to be okay."

María opened her mouth to answer just as the first bomb went off.

The papers said later there were seven bombs in all, but Ricardo only heard the first one. Actually, the blast knocked the table over and he only heard the explosion as he and María and Sophi went flying toward the ground. He told me later that that first bomb must have been hidden around the Security area near where they were sitting, and because it was so near, the air was instantly full of flying glass, debris, and dust. One minute he was sitting there looking at María and the next thing he knew he was on the ground, his ears were ringing, and he couldn't breathe. He heard María scream. He started coughing and lifted his head and looked to see her scrambling on all fours over to where Sophi was laying. Blood was streaming from glass cuts on María's arms and legs. Ricardo looked at Sophi. Sophi was moving and looking around but not crying, just stunned. María reached Sophi and scooped her into her arms, and then Sophi started to wail. María was on her knees just holding Sophi and trying to get her balance. People were running all around and screaming. Ricardo started to pull himself off the ground. That is when he saw the gunman.

We know now of course, that this was a well-planned and coordinated attack, involving six terrorists. But of course, at the time, Ricardo only knew what he saw. But as soon as he saw the gunman running down the corridor shooting people, he knew what was happening. In that concourse there were two gunmen, one of whom was in the hallway that Ricardo was in. People were running and screaming, and the gunman was chasing them, mowing them down with his automatic rifle. Because all the simultaneous attacks happened on the outside of the security zone, the terrorists were able to smuggle all those machine guns and hand grenades into the airport. There were plenty of people standing at the check-in counters, or picking up baggage at baggage claim, all of them just sitting ducks, and very few counterterrorist police around. I believe the final death count was eighty.

Ah, here we are, my little abode. Hang on, this key always gives me trouble. Here we go. Come on in.

Let me get the lights. Well, thank you. Yes, the place is larger than it looks from the outside. Have a seat and make yourself comfortable. Let me see what I have in the wine department here. Hmmm... Cabernet? No... hmm, I thought I had another box... is this it? Ah, yes... yes, here it is... Do you like Pinot? I've been waiting for an occasion to open this Pinot. Ah, good, then let's try it. Here we go. Here's a glass for you and one for me. Salud.

Hmm, not bad, not bad. How is it for you? I like a Pinot occasionally. Where was I? Oh yes, well... from the time the first bomb went off and Ricardo got shot, probably only six seconds elapsed. The blast knocked him to the ground; he lifted his head up to see María scramble over to Sophi; he saw María on her knees holding Sophi; he heard the gunshots and the screams; he saw the gunman shooting people; he saw the people falling; there was blood everywhere; and he just lunged up and threw himself over María and Sophi, trying to cover them up, just as the bullets hit all three of them, and they all fell to the ground. Ricardo caught two bullets, one in his shoulder and the one that creased his skull and knocked him out. María and Sophi, as you know, were not so lucky, and they both were probably killed instantly. Of course it was the photograph of María and Sophi lying there dead and covered in blood under Ricardo's arms that made all the papers and became the icon of that attack—yes, those are Ricardo's arms in that photo—I don't know how it is that photographers are allowed to get into a crime scene like that so fast and take pictures, but that one picture came to symbolize that horrible day. That terrible image of María holding Sophi, and all that blood. At some point, after the gunmen were all killed, and the rescuers came in, they realized that Ricardo was still alive, and rushed him to the hospital. He was covered in blood, his blood and María's and Sophi's. It's probably a good thing he never saw that. The bullet to his head had fractured his skull but had not entered his brain. Still the doctors were concerned about brain swelling. My understanding is that they kept him on ice and in some sort of induced coma. Anyway, on the third day they brought him out of the coma. They didn't want to tell him about María and Sophi when he asked because they weren't sure if María was his wife, or daughter, or how they were related. Only when they discovered that they had just recently met, did they tell Ricardo that both María and Sophi were dead.

No, you're right, it's really a horribly sad story. Most of the things that happen to us are sad, and all the ways we die are horrible, but they rarely are as savage as that day was... We all know, intellectually of course, that death can come for us anytime, but when we actually see it up close... well, we're just not prepared for it. Nothing prepares us for it.

Ricardo? Well, he spent a few weeks in the hospital. I went down and visited him there during that first week he was recuperating. He was still in pretty bad shape then. He told me he couldn't accept the fact that María and Sophi were just *gone*—that they just didn't exist anymore. They finally released him from the hospital after three weeks and he flew back to Panama. Well, actually, he took the train to Barcelona and flew out of there—he just couldn't face going back to the Madrid airport. I don't know if he ever will really recover from it... no, no I mean emotionally. Physically, he recovered. But emotionally, I don't know. He wrote me recently and said that the only way he is able to cope is to try and do one nice thing every day for someone. But he expressed it in a rather odd way. He said that what he had learned from the whole experience was that the best we can do in this world is to try and love other people and to try and let them love us... I thought it was an odd way to phrase it—almost as if we're incapable of love but we have to try anyway... I'll have to write him and ask him about that... I heard from some friends that he does some volunteering down at the little school in the town where he lives in Panama... Maybe that helps him... But he did mention that he was starting to write again. I think that's a good sign. That's the thing about him and writing, you know—it's some kind of exorcism. Maybe it's that way for all writers, I don't know. Is it that way for you? Interesting. Yes, well, maybe one day you can meet him. I think you would like him—he's an interesting man.

But anyway... since you asked last night, that's the story of how Ricardo happened to end up in the Madrid airport on that day when the bombings happen. Well, you're very welcome. Bathroom? Oh it's just down that hallway, on the left.

Ah you're back. What? Ah yes, you noticed that little room? Oh yes, that's my little playroom. Yes, it's nicely stocked. Come on, I'll give you the tour. Yes, the bed is huge—I had to have it specially built, but I wanted it big enough to hold at least four people. Notice the large steel eyelets on the side of the frame? Those are for tie-downs... and here are the leather straps. See how soft they are?

You know, my friend, there are times when it's important to be completely forthright and honest... totally honest... And I know it's been a long evening... but it wasn't by mere happenchance that we ended up back here... So tell me, my friend, would you be interested in being tied down? Because I would be very interested in tying you down and playing with you... maybe even fucking you. You wouldn't have to do anything... Yes, well of course, safe sex. Yes, I thought you might. Come, let me show you this, behind this mirror—a walk-in closet full of outfits. Oh, yes, I'm sure I have your size. Yes that one's nice... What do you think of this one? Uh huh, I understand. Of course. Well, we'll talk about the rules, but first, pick out a nice outfit. Here, in this drawer are some bras. Well, I understand, but there's a first time for everything. Besides, we're just playing, and you're completely safe here. Now take off your shirt and try this one on. Ah, yes, that's nice, very nice. Hmm... how about this top? And this little dress? It's okay. Yes, put your pants on the chair there. Hmm... no, forget the dress, just put these panties on. Yes, that's good. Now, put this leather collar around your neck. Here, I'll tie it for you. Now, let's see. Oh yes, very nice, very very nice.

Ok, come over here to the bed. Lie down. I'm just going to tie your wrists down. We can stop anytime you want. Here we go. See? Not too bad, eh? Now, I'm just going to put just a little make-up on you... No, no, it washes off easily, I promise. We'll start with little lipstick...a little blush... good... and just a touch of eye shadow... hold still... ah, yes... you look beautiful. Let's see how those lips taste... Ah good. Now let's see what's in my playbox here... some lubricant, yes, condoms, yes... Oh, look at these dildos... I'll start with the small one, just to warm you up. Well, I guess I'd better get undressed. This will be fun. You know, I always say, you meet the nicest people in Belgian bars.

-fin-